Praise for *You'll Be The Death Of Me*

5 Angels! Recommended Read! "…Ms. Wolf has done a fantastic job of bringing the romance to the reader, hooking you from page one. Ms. Wolf's sense of humor is fantastic and will have you laughing until you cry. Everything you need for the perfect romance and so much more is here: great characters, laugh out loud scenes and a little bit of love.… You'll be the Death of Me is a wonderful book that I would recommend to everyone." ~ *Sonya, Fallen Angel Reviews*

"This is an amusing story. I found it to be highly entertaining and very well written. It is enjoyable to see romance not always being taken too seriously. I look forward to seeing more works by Ms. Wolf and highly recommend You'll be the Death of Me. In my opinion, it would be a great addition to anyone's collection." ~ *Karen Magill, Reviewer for Coffee Time Romances*

"I really enjoyed You'll Be the Death of Me, with its quirky sense of humor and its cast of appealing characters. Ms. Wolf has a quirky sense of humor, which makes the story light-hearted as well as hopeful. Immediately I found myself rooting for Allison and Jay, both of whom have allowed negative relationship experiences to ice over their hearts. This is one of those books where the reader just wants the characters to achieve their goals and the dreams close to their hearts." ~ *Annie for Joyfully Reviewed*

You'll Be The Death Of Me

By Stacia Wolf

A SAṁHAIN PUBLISHING, LTD. publication.

Samhain Publishing, Ltd.
2932 Ross Clark Circle, #384
Dothan, AL 36301
www.samhainpublishing.com

You'll Be The Death Of Me
Copyright © 2006 by Stacia Wolf
Print ISBN: 1-59998-265-X
Digital ISBN: 1-59998-039-8
Cover by Scott Carpenter

First Samhain Publishing, Ltd. electronic publication: June 2006
First Samhain Publishing, Ltd. print publication: September 2006

Dedication

For most of my life, I've had dreams. Sometimes those dreams were set aside for greater things, like family, love, cares and needs of the day. But the dreams persisted and with much help I've realized most of them. Today, one strong, seemed-impossible-to-reach fantasy is reality. So here is a partial list of who helped me succeed.

Thanks to my on-line writing compatriots for helping me hone my skills to the point where my writing made sense. And for cheering me on when it seemed hopeless.

Thanks especially to Heather Rae, who unselfishly and compassionately shared her new-found success by telling me about an emerging and exciting publishing company, and even telling me what manuscript to submit. Rae, you're the best.

To Jazzy, who although you've left this life, will always inspire me to write about little cranky dogs with a big heart filled with love.

To Joan, who's the sister I never had and the best friend anyone could want.

My kids – thank you for loving the maniacal writer-woman who takes your mom's place from time-to-time, and for cheering me on.

Mom and Dad, thanks for instilling in me at a young age determination to get the job done, and for always believing that I could reach the sky.

This is for you.

Chapter One

Molly Downs was dead. The DNA of the body found at the bottom of the ravine matched that of a hair taken from her hairbrush. The whereabouts of the famous actress, missing for months, were no longer a mystery. But one question remained: who had killed her? As Detective Ben Stark gazed about the room, looking from the shocked boyfriend to the estranged mother crying crocodile tears, only Allison Leavitt's emotions rang true. She swiped at the hot tears that coursed down her cheeks.

Oh, why did she always cry? Why couldn't she keep her stupid emotions under control? One would think that after killing off at least fifty victims, she'd be immune to all of this, handling it like any other facet of her chosen career. But, no, once again she sat there blubbering like a child.

Saving the latest chapter of her current murder-mystery, Allison —known as the reclusive author 'Al Leavitt' to 'his' many fans—shut the computer off in resignation. Long experience had taught her that writing would be impossible until she calmed down her over-sensitive nerves. Snuffling deeply, she reached to turn off the lamp.

Boom! Splat!

Something smacked her shoulder with a hard sting, and tiny flecks of red scattered across the darkened computer screen. Out of the corner of her eye, she glimpsed a dark figure fleeing into the night through her partially open French doors.

Instinctively her hand flew to her back, tangling in her hair; pulling it back, she found it smeared with red. She'd been shot! Standing up, she let out a horrendous screech and waited for her world to darken, her life to fade away.

Instead, she heard a giggle. She pivoted around and her gaze flew to the figure standing in the apartment doorway. She instantly recognized Paige Hilton, her best friend and the major bane of her life. Allison's spare key twirled about her index finger.

Holding out her blood-red hand, Allison whispered, "I'm shot."

"Relax. It's only paint," Paige told her dryly.

Allison felt her eyes widen as she tried to understand. Her usually quick mind refused to work. "Paint? Why would I bleed paint?"

Guffawing, Paige entered the room. "You aren't bleeding, dummy. It's a paint ball! Water-based paint, by the way. Cleans right up. When you told me yesterday that you were killing Molly off tonight, I remembered how you always get so depressed when a character dies. I thought I'd distract you with your own murder."

"My own murder?" Flicking an amber curl from her face, Allison could only stare at her friend.

"What are you tonight, a parrot? Yes, your own murder, and there are clues. It's up to you to find out who killed you."

A game. Paige was playing a game with her. As comprehension sank in, a huge grin lit Allison's face. This could be precisely what she needed to break this silly funk.

"That does sound like fun. Where do I start?"

Paige went through the French doors and out into the illuminated courtyard. "The pool, of course. Where else would a good mystery begin?"

🐈 🐈 🐈

"I heard her scream," Birdie Talbot, Jay 's landlady, repeated for the fifth time in the last two minutes, her voice wobbly with tears. "And her door was ajar. Allison never leaves her door unlocked. Part of writing murder mysteries, I suppose. Makes you paranoid. When I looked in, I could see blood! Blood everywhere!" She clutched Ping, the mottled brown-and-white mutt that she insisted was a valuable Chinese Crested show dog. The animal responded by sneezing all over Jay. The bell on the strange little dog's fat blue velvet collar jingled; a matching blue cap sat precariously on its head, held on by an elastic band.

Detective Jay Cantrall wiped off the dog's offending spray as he followed the surprisingly swift, rotund woman toward the door that his mysterious next-door neighbor hid behind. He'd lived there for a week and had yet to see her. She never seemed to come out of her apartment, but he heard noises from time to time. Music, not too loud, and sometimes thumps, like maybe she was exercising or perhaps something more…primal than that.

He couldn't think about that now; his cop instincts kicked in strongly, telling him that something fishy was going on. Something didn't seem right.

"We're so lucky you're here. A police officer in our building now—can you imagine? Allison lives next door to a police officer and still—" She began that strange warbling cry again. Mrs. Talbot might feel lucky, but Jay didn't share her sentiment. As for the police officer in the building—Jay's partner, Pearce, had lived here for over a year.

They arrived at Allison's partially opened door. Mrs. Talbot waved him through, her chin wobbling dramatically as her expansive bosom heaved under her bright pink and turquoise muumuu. "I can't go in there," she warbled. "When I think about that poor child—oh, I just can't."

Jay tamped down his irritation with her dramatics. Being a cop included dealing with witnesses. This particular witness bordered on hysteria; becoming harsh with her wouldn't accomplish a thing. He forced his lips into a reassuring smile that he hoped didn't look as phony as it felt.

"That's fine. You wait here and I'll take a look around, okay?" At her nod, he turned away and entered the darkened apartment. As soon as he left her, he reached to the small of his back and pulled out the revolver he'd hidden there when she'd summoned him. No use taking any chances.

The empty room's décor didn't seem typical of a woman. A lone lamp at the computer desk and a matching floor lamp near the open French doors were the only illumination. Instead of fluffy, floral furniture, frilly knick-knacks and pastel artwork, it was decorated starkly. A black futon with pillows in various shades of silver graced one wall; a smoky glass and wrought-iron coffee table sported only a few magazines. Narrow glass shelving covered another wall, displaying a massive collection of Hot Wheels, many still in the original packages.

Walking fully into the apartment, he couldn't miss what Mrs. Talbot had described—bloody streaks on the polished wooden floor surrounding the computer desk. He could tell that point of impact had occurred a couple of feet above the desk; he saw splatters as far as the tiled kitchen floor about a dozen feet away. Not wanting to disturb any evidence, he didn't approach the area.

A single trail of footprints went through the blood, heading toward the French doors. The victim's, or the attacker's? Had to be the victim's, since he saw no drag marks of any sort. Could she still be alive? His heart accelerated at the thought. *There might still be time.*

But his feet didn't move. Frowning, he looked at the crime scene one more time. Something wasn't right.

The smell. That sickening metallic smell of fresh blood. It didn't coil his stomach; that familiar feeling was absent. Kneeling down, he touched the blood gingerly and brought his finger to his nose.

Paint.

Cursing under his breath, he wondered what kind of prank he'd been pulled into. At that instant, two figures burst through the French doors, laughter announcing their entrance.

Leaping to his feet, Jay pointed his gun at the intruders. They stopped instantly; one gave a shriek of fright, while the other stared at him, mouth opening and closing, guppy style.

His breath caught in his throat at the sight of her. Even hidden under a baggy shirt and shorts, Jay couldn't help but appreciate her lush figure. It reminded him of a curvy 1940's-era pin-up girl. Impossibly blue eyes surrounded by creamy skin and framed by a riot of ginger-colored curls coiled his stomach all right, but in a different manner than what he'd expected when Mrs. Talbot had first asked him for help. *Nope, this was pure sexual tension, a recognition that reached every cell in his being, every pore—*

Damn, he needed some time off. Thoughts like that didn't belong in his head while on the job.

The other woman, tall and model-slim with long, dark hair, olive skin and amber eyes, croaked out, "Who are you?"

Fancy forgotten, he narrowed his eyes. "Jay Cantrall. L.A....no, sorry. Spokane Police. And you are?"

Her companion finally controlled her guppy imitation but didn't say a word. Beautiful, but dumb. Then he noticed it.

A drop of red paint fell from her long hair down onto her white T-shirt with 'How Big ARE the Grand Tetons?' emblazoned on it. The paint landed on the photo of a mountain, right on the summit.

This must be Allison Leavitt, the writer. Disappointing, in a way. He'd hoped for someone brilliant, who could share some witty banter with him. He couldn't imagine fish-face here carrying on any sort of conversation. Her books couldn't be very exciting, either, which was probably why he'd never heard of her.

"I'm Paige Hilton," the brunette told him. "I live in 2B. This is Allison Leavitt; this is her apartment." Her brows arched in an unspoken question. He quickly answered it.

"Mrs. Talbot heard a scream, saw what she thought was blood and called me."

"You must have been close to get here so fast," Paige said. "Allison didn't get paint-balled more than five minutes ago."

"I live next door, just moved in." He studied the women, trying to get a hold on what had just happened in the apartment. "Is this some kind of a practical joke?" Recognizing that the two were no threat, Jay put away his gun. Neither woman replied.

He felt Paige's eyes travel over him, taking in his tanned legs, which were exposed by the rumpled khaki shorts he'd donned after work in an effort to beat the stifling July heat. Who knew that Spokane temperatures could rival Los Angeles? He knew his hair looked disheveled and his plain white tank top was untucked; he'd been lying on the couch watching an old Humphrey Bogart movie when Mrs. Talbot had knocked on his door.

He didn't like being on display. Paige's look of appreciation bothered him. But not as much as Allison Leavitt's unbreakable stare.

Shaking his head slightly, he tried again to get an answer. "Can either of you tell me what's going on here?" His hand waved over the paint-spattered mess.

"Oh, that!" Elbowing her immobile friend in the side, Paige shrugged. "Al here gets a bit depressed whenever she kills off a character, and I decided to distract her by staging her own murder.

Actually it was a hit-and-run paintball attack," Paige laughed lightly. "Right now we're collecting clues to figure out who shot her." Grasping her friend's wrist, she lifted Allison's hand to display a saltshaker.

Jay's eyebrows rose. A paintball murder? With a saltshaker as a clue? What type of whackos lived in this building? He'd known he would regret moving in here, but he'd been desperate for a place to stay, and his new partner, Pearce Randolph, had helped him snag the apartment. Now he knew why it had been available. He suppressed a snort. The former tenants had probably fled the insanity.

All right, back to business. He didn't have a crime here, unless lunacy counted. Time for him to leave.

"Well, ladies, nice to meet you. I'll leave you to finish your 'game.'" And he could head back to catch the end of that Bogart movie. *Those* characters he understood. This pair was beyond him. Even though he found 'Al' incredibly fetching, it took more than good looks to intrigue him. With a forced smile, he turned to go.

"Wait." Allison Leavitt's quiet, husky voice sounded exactly like Lauren Bacall from *The Maltese Falcon*: low, sensual, like malt liquor over tumbled ice cubes. Turning around, he faced those baby blue eyes once more. And found himself sinking again.

"You're a cop, right? I mean, of course you are, that's what you said. Do you think you could help me solve my murder? I mean, watching your mind work through this would be great!"

As she spoke, her hands danced, emphasizing her words. His gaze followed the tiny showers of salt that escaped from the shaker she held. She caught his gaze, then the flying salt, and set the shaker down with a *thunk* on the coffee table. Touches of color tinged her high cheeks. Damn, he was a sucker for a woman who blushed.

Stacia Wolf

But that didn't mean he wanted to get caught up in some crazy scheme of theirs. Insane people usually led to trouble, and he'd had enough of that to last a lifetime.

"I'll think I'll pass. Thanks anyway." With a wave of his hand, he headed out the door.

Chapter Two

"What's wrong with you?" Paige hissed at Allison. "Why did you choose now to imitate a rock?" Pausing at the door, she turned back toward Allison. "I'll try to bring him back, but you have to promise me that you won't do a repeat performance, okay?"

With that she disappeared.

"Paige, wait!" But her friend didn't reappear, either not hearing her or choosing not to respond. Probably the latter.

Allison raised a shaking hand to her forehead. Had she really seen what she thought she saw? Was her books' hero, Ben Stark, actually living in this apartment complex? It couldn't be a mistake; she'd carried a mental image of him around for over six years now.

It was him, in the flesh, every hard-muscled, delectable inch of him. How could it be? She'd dreamed him up herself; there was no way he could be a real-life man!

Panic and excitement battled inside her. Ben Stark had, over the years, become her ideal man. She even thought of him and those rugged-yet-elegant hands when she 'serviced' herself. In fact, he'd become so integral to her sexual fantasies that anymore, she couldn't get started without thinking of him.

And now she'd met someone who fit her every thought of him, right down to the soft silver eyes that showed no emotion yet held secrets that women could only dream of. He—

Knock it off, Al. She snorted at herself for having illicit thoughts over a man who looked like her fictional fantasy hero. How crazy was that?

Only she'd held that image in her head since the moment she'd imagined Ben Stark into existence. It had been so strong that she'd never wavered from it. Every attempt by an artist to capture him had never quite worked, so her book covers had never shown him.

Except her upcoming one. This last artist had carefully listened to every word she'd said about Ben. The final result sat in a large envelope by the computer. Crossing over to it, she whisked it out to study it once again, hoping that she was wrong, that Jay Cantrall looked nothing like Ben Stark.

No such luck. She could almost believe that Jay had posed for this cover. A bareheaded Ben stood in the rain, an evidence bag that contained a knife dangling from one hand. He gazed down at the body at his feet while someone drew a white line about the corpse. From the unkempt blond hair to the chiseled chin and the sensual lips that showed little hint of humor, it captured her ideal of what Ben Stark would look like. Long, lean, hungry, driven. And devastatingly handsome. The rendering also fit Jay to a T.

Except he was sexier as a living, breathing male than she'd imagined Ben could ever be. She couldn't write that much sensuality into a book—the words simply didn't exist. Oh, yeah, her knees were jelly just thinking about Jay's long, elegant fingers wrapped around his gun. She shivered at the thought of those hands touching her.

Tiny red flecks fell from her hair, miraculously missing the artwork in her hands. It was only a copy, but she didn't want it ruined. Slipping the cover into the envelope, she dashed to the bathroom, intent on washing the paint off her.

She took off of her shirt and bra, then turned on the tub faucet and stuck her head under it. Cool water sluiced over her hair; adding some shampoo, she watched brilliant red hues pool in the tub. As the color disappeared down the drain, she wished she could do the same with her thoughts about the handsome cop she'd just met.

The last thing Allison Leavitt needed in her life was a man. No, thank you, she would pass on that entrée! *Been there, done that, got the T-shirt.* Men were good for only one thing: sex. And she didn't need any of that. She'd never enjoyed it and didn't have to experience it again to remind her of that fact.

Here she was, almost thirty, and no man had ever given her an orgasm. Not only that, but she'd never experienced the sparks that Paige always talked about. She must be frigid. Either that, or men were terribly inadequate to meet her needs.

She found the rest of the male package to be lamentable as well. In the past several years, after the questionable sex, every guy had suddenly expected her to support him in the manner to which he wanted to become accustomed. If she didn't pay for every dinner, he'd pout. If she refused to buy something for him while they shopped, she'd get a cold stare for hours. Hints of cruises or sporting event tickets, and in one case, new wheels for his car, had been added to the already bleak deal.

Did guys think that because she was a published author, her brain had stopped functioning? Why would she ever think paying some lazy male's way would be a good idea? She remembered the pain her last relationship had put her through. Nick had left her with a very bad taste in her mouth concerning men and sex.

At first, he'd been perfect. His devotion to her had touched her deeply; he'd been loving and very supportive. He'd claimed to have fallen for her at first sight.

After a few months, he'd convinced her to allow him to move in, then somehow had suckered her into paying almost all the bills. After he'd lined up another 'sugar mama,' he'd left her. But that had happened only after she'd insisted he started paying his own way.

Apparently, being self-sufficient had never entered into his plans. No, Nick made a living at being a parasite, and his best asset seemed to be coercing women into believing his lies.

And Allison had fallen for it. *Stupid, stupid, stupid.* How an intelligent woman could be so easily fooled by empty words of love and devotion, she'd never know. But she'd learned her lesson, and she'd learned it well.

Never again would she subject herself to that. Men wanted only one thing from her: money. She wasn't attractive or exciting enough to hold a man's attention on her own. Besides, she'd soon be thirty and that was way past the age of cuteness. No, she didn't need another reminder of her shortcomings.

Then why did you react that way to Jay Cantrall? He'd surprised her, that was all. Her request that he help her solve Paige's 'mystery' stemmed from that, as well. She'd reacted to the shock at finding 'Ben Stark' standing in her living room. Yes, that explained it. No way could she be interested in anything more!

The water ran clear now, just like her thoughts. Allison turned the faucet off, wrapped a towel about her head and put her bra back on. She left her shirt lying where she'd tossed it and instead, went to her bedroom. She took an oversized black tank top from the closet, perfect for the muggy July heat.

Slipping it on, she rubbed her hair vigorously with the towel, then ran a comb through, smoothing down the wet curls. She twisted most of the strands to the top of her head and secured them in place with a plain black clip.

Glancing in the bedroom's full-length mirror on her way to the living room, she noted with satisfaction that her loose black shorts didn't look any worse for the wear. She didn't linger on her abundant curves; she knew she'd never be model slim, and had resigned herself years ago to the fact her figure would never be ideal.

"Al! Are you ready?" Paige's voice floated through the open door. Allison poked her head out into the hallway and saw her friend emerge from the apartment next door, tugging a very reluctant-looking Jay behind her. Paige's eyes lit up when she caught sight of her.

"Jay's agreed to help you solve your mystery. Isn't that great? You need to collect a few more clues, then we'll meet with all the suspects in the rec room, okay?"

Allison's heart plummeted. Paige didn't mean to leave her alone with him, did she? Jay's mere presence short-circuited what many thought to be a very sharp mind. No, she couldn't face that again—she didn't like looking like a thoughtless ninny in front of the too-attractive detective.

Sending a glare Paige's way, she asked her, "Could I talk to you for a moment? Alone?" She tossed Jay an apologetic smile. His raised brows and lack of an answering grin told her that she didn't impress him with her behavior.

Tough. She smelled another of Paige's matchmaking antics. Paige claimed to be very happy with her life as a single woman, but seemed determined to find partners for all her friends. But Allison didn't want a man.

Not even one as delectable as Jay Cantrall.

Tugging her friend into her apartment, she whispered, "What are you up to? I don't want to be alone with him!"

Paige's eyes widened. "Who wouldn't want to be with such a dish? Al, he's gorgeous! Don't tell me you didn't notice that? Or was your stupor caused by his good looks?"

"My 'stupor,' as you call it, wasn't because of Jay's looks. At least not in the way you think. Look!" Allison whipped out the cover art. It only took Paige a moment to come to the same conclusion Allison had. She stared at the artwork in shock.

"That's Jay! Al, why is Jay on your book cover? I thought you just met him!"

"I did just meet him. This is some strange coincidence."

"A coincidence? This could be his twin! How on earth did Jay end up on your book cover?" Paige stared at the painting; Allison could swear she drooled—literally—over it.

"That's not Jay! It's just some freak chance thing. Now that I've met him, I'll have to have it altered." She couldn't have this go to print. Jay could sue her for using his image. She needed to call her publisher and ask about the signed release from whoever had modeled for the cover.

"You can't do that! This is the sweetest cover you've had yet! Oh, Al, can't you get his permission or something?"

Get his permission. Allison couldn't see the gruff, sour man allowing his likeness to grace the cover of one of her books. Even one guaranteed to be a best seller. This one, Ben Stark's eighth, would hold two twists: his long-time partner, Emily Hayes, would become the latest victim of a serial killer, and he would finally find the missing, mysterious lover he'd been searching for through the last few books. It would be a poignant story, and knowing this, Allison's stack of tissue boxes contained two new additions.

No, she wouldn't ask Jay Cantrall's permission. She didn't want him to know he was the exact image of her dream man, the man she'd spent the last several years with, in her fantasies at least. Jay didn't need to know that. In fact, nobody needed to know that. It'd always been her secret, and it would remain that way for eternity, as long as Allison was concerned.

"No, Paige, not going to happen. And I don't want to solve my murder with him. I don't think he knows how to crack a smile, let alone enjoy something fun like this."

"You're such a drag. Can't you see his potential? He just needs someone to show him the exciting things in life."

Allison smiled skeptically. "And you think that's supposed to be me? The last thing I need right now is a man! Honestly, Paige! Wasn't finding Pearce a girlfriend enough for you?"

Paige and Detective Pearce Randolph had dated after he'd moved into Cedar Boughs Apartments. After their break-up, Paige had been determined to prove that she was over him, so much so that she'd started matchmaking for him. Right when Pearce had declared his desire to strangle her, she had done the impossible and produced his dream woman. Now it appeared that she planned on doing the same thing for Allison.

"That's the point, Al. Deadlines always tie you up in knots. You need to relax and enjoy life more. Perhaps Jay's the right one to help you. You can't judge every man by the jerks you've met in the past." She flicked a finger toward the cover art. "Don't you think that this cover is a sign?"

A sign. The last time Allison had believed in fate was with Nick, when he'd told her that their meeting had been written in the stars. She'd ended up with hundreds of dollars in calls racked up on her cell phone from Nick to his new lover. Not to mention her broken heart.

Nope, no more signs for her. Those days of acting on impulse were over. Look at what she'd accomplished by sticking to a goal: seven best-selling books, a fat bank account and the freedom to do what she wanted, when she wanted. And she would, too. Just as soon as she made the next deadline.

"Paige," she held up her hand, halting her friend's cascading words. "I'll go find all your clues and solve this mystery, just like you want. And if Jay Cantrall decides to tag along, great, he's welcome. But please don't take any of this as a sign that something's going to happen between us. Because that's not even a remote possibility."

"Allison, you can't throw away this opportunity. Haven't you ever wondered what it would be like if Ben Stark were a real guy? And here he is. Right out of a fantasy. Maybe you could indulge in a little fantasy of your own."

Startled, Allison locked gazes with Paige. How did she know that images of Ben filled up many of her nights? Did she have a crystal ball?

Maybe you could indulge...

She shook her head, denying the allure of such an idea. She wouldn't think of Jay that way. Besides, considering his cool demeanor, what made her think that he'd be any better at sex than any of the others she'd been with?

"No, Paige, it's not going to happen. And I'd appreciate it if you stop playing matchmaker, all right?"

Paige nodded in agreement, but her mouth twitched slightly, and she failed to meet Allison's gaze. Allison slanted her a disbelieving look. That was way too easy. She didn't trust Paige when it took this little effort.

Chapter Three

They stepped out into the hallway where Jay waited for them. Birdie Talbot, complete with Ping hanging majestically over her arm, regaled Jay with her earlier scare.

"All that blood everywhere—you can imagine my horror thinking that poor sweet Allison was dead! Oh, Allison, there you are! Thank heavens you're fine. Paige…" She turned reproachful eyes on the younger woman. "How could you not tell me what you were up to? You caused me such a fright!"

Paige's smile barely surpassed a grimace. "Birdie, I did tell you yesterday, when I asked if we could use the rec room for tonight. In fact, I invited you, remember?"

Birdie Talbot blinked. "Did you?" Her face brightened. "Oh, that's right, you did! Is that tonight? Oh, how silly I am!" She tittered softly, glancing at Jay. "I do hope you forgive me. Sometimes I'm so scatterbrained!"

Jay's face gave away nothing. "No harm done." He eyed the tiny dog with misgiving, however. Allison couldn't help but smile. Ping was definitely a sight to behold. Wearing an outlandish blue velvet sailor suit, complete with a miniature cap, Ping definitely didn't blend into the background. His pale, blond crest poked out at outlandish angles; his hairless brown skin was accentuated by small white spots. The constantly jingling bell sewn into the collar didn't help.

His attitude stood out, as well. Very regal and aloof, Ping didn't like most people. And he loved to show his disdain.

Birdie hugged Allison with her free arm. "I'm so happy you're okay! Oh, that reminds me! A package came for you today. I held it for you. I know how you hate your writing to be interrupted. Let me go get it for you." She looked at her pet in frustration. "I can't carry both the package and Ping. And with the doors open, I can't let him run around. He got out yesterday and it took me forever to find him. Here!" Thrusting Ping at Paige, Birdie scurried off to her apartment on the other side of Allison's.

Paige held Ping at arm's length; the dog didn't take well to her, either. Growling with more bravado than a tiny dog should contain, he snapped at her fingers, apparently ignoring the fact that she held him four feet off the ground. With a shudder of dislike, Paige plopped the disagreeable animal onto the carpet. "There, you little freak!"

Ping growled, glaring at Paige. Paige turned her attention back to Allison, handing her a folded piece of paper. "Here's a list of the clues. You have twenty minutes. When you've collected all of them, come to the rec room. We'll be waiting."

Waggling her fingers, she rushed down the hallway to the sound of Ping's angry barking.

Ping sat down against the wall, his upper lip curling at his remaining companions. Under Birdie's supervision, Ping had the run of the complex. Outside, she kept him securely fenced inside the pool and garden area. He was her beloved baby; she didn't take any chances. Allison sighed; apparently she was dog-sitting.

Allison knew better than to try picking Ping up in his current cranky mood. Most of the time, she got along quite well with the dog. She'd learned from past experience, however, not to bother him when he acted grumpy. She didn't relish being nipped.

She smiled apologetically at Jay. "We'll have to wait here until Birdie gets back. It shouldn't be long. In the meantime, we can study Paige's clues." She unfolded the paper, holding it in front of her.

He moved toward her; she could feel his reluctance, tempered with his determination. She didn't know if he truly wanted to participate or if he was merely trying to be polite. Well, time would tell. Not that she wanted to find out; his good looks and her strong reaction to him made her all the more leery of him. It didn't matter that he looked like her image of Ben Stark. He wasn't Ben, and she needed to keep that in mind.

Maybe you could indulge.

No. She forced her mind back into the game. She didn't need any indulgence with this man. She'd just ignore his looks, and the smell of his after-shave that left her somewhat light-headed and breathless.

With one eye on the dog and the other on Paige's list, she read the clues, taking care to keep her voice sure and steady. "'Flavors food and is often found in large bodies of water.' Okay, that's the salt. I found it by the pool." The heat from his body pelted her. A wave of longing swept over her: what would it be like if his body grazed hers? Did he feel the magnetic pull, too?

Her voice faltered. She forced herself to continue.

"The next clue is: 'It thrives in the tropics, and loves moist heat.' That's easy; we'll have to check out the sauna." She looked up at Jay to find him looking not at her or at Paige's clues, but down at his foot. Down where Ping's bell jingled madly. His face was twisted in disbelief and dismay; Ping had wrapped himself around Jay's leg and—

"Omigosh!" Allison exclaimed, horrified. "Ping! No! Bad dog!"

Ping ignored Allison's cries. The bell only jangled louder as Jay shook his foot, trying to dislodge the dog.

"Ping! No!" Birdie Talbot's reprimand distracted Ping just as Jay gave a mighty shake of his foot. The upward swing of his leg sent the dog flying up, up, up and into Birdie's outstretched arms. Allison's package hit the ground with a thump.

The rotund woman pulled herself straight, outrage reddening her features as she glared at Jay. "How dare you punt my Ping!"

Chapter Four

Embarrassed beyond measure, Jay collected the clues for Allison's 'mystery' with an intensity that would have been more fitting in an actual murder investigation. At first the game had sounded harmless. Now, after the 'punting' incident, it descended to the same level as extracting one's own teeth.

It didn't ease his humiliation to have Allison tagging along. Her misty beauty grated on his self-control. If anything, her attempts to smooth things over and put him at ease were setting his nerves on edge because he'd discovered something about Allison; something that he wished he didn't know.

She was a toucher.

Her long sensuous fingers would skim over his shoulder as she spoke; she would give his arm a reassuring squeeze. Each time she moved close, an irresistible floral scent would tantalize him. His libido was going insane; it took all his willpower to keep himself from 'rising' to the occasion. He tried to stay aloof, to hold back, but for some sadistic reason, that only encouraged her to reach out and touch him more. Did she know what she was doing to him?

Of course she did. No woman who looked like her, smelled like her and smiled like her could be unaware of the effect she had on men. She must be getting some perverse pleasure in knowing she attracted him.

Yet when she looked at him with that delicious smile on her face, he could see no hint of satisfaction or gloating in her demeanor. She seemed completely without guile.

He didn't buy it. He'd been sucked in by that level of 'innocence' before. He didn't plan on falling for it again. His naiveté concerning women like her was the reason he'd wound up in Spokane instead of remaining in his native Los Angeles.

The trouble with being a celebrity's twin, Jay reasoned, was the people who'd do anything to meet the celebrity. Jay's brother, Jeff, a minor television star in the States, had recently become the rage on a British soap opera. The more Jeff's popularity grew, the faster Jay's anonymity shrank.

Jay's last romantic interest, Melanie, had not only turned out to be married to an assistant district attorney, but she'd nursed an obsession with Jay's brother as well. She'd kept hinting about meeting his family, especially his brother. When Jay became suspicious and put the brakes on, she'd broken it off with him.

Months later, the affair had come to light, and the ensuing scandal had prompted his transfer to Spokane. Officially, he was here to help shut down a car smuggling ring that originated in L.A. and now had expanded to Spokane. Unofficially, he'd pissed off his boss by being caught with the wife of a prominent member of the political circle that inhabited the L.A. legal system.

His transfer messed with his plans for a promotion from detective to lieutenant. He'd been so close, he knew, and now his promotion was put on hold until his return. When that would be, remained up in the air. He understood, however, that if he walked away from this case with an impressive outcome, it would not only get him home faster, but could help his dreams of advancement. To do that, he needed to stay focused on his job.

No, Jay didn't plan on getting sucked in again by someone pretending to be so sweetly innocent while hiding a secret agenda. He'd learned the hard way that women preferred his brother. He didn't need another lesson to remind him.

In what seemed an eternity, but in truth, only lasted about fifteen minutes, they found all the clues: a silk orchid, a small green Hot Wheels car, a glass jar filled with what looked like fish, a burgundy wax birthday candle in the shape of the number two and, of course, the saltshaker. None of it made any sense to Jay, but he hoped they meant something to Allison.

They walked to the rec room, located near the pool and next to the exercise room. The Boughs, an upper-scale apartment complex, was well furnished with many amenities. The rec room boasted a full kitchen, big screen television and space enough for a dance floor. It could be accessed, like everything else, with a special key that only residents possessed. Mrs. Talbot liked to brag that her apartments were the best maintained and the most pleasant in all of Spokane. So far, Jay hadn't experienced the 'pleasant' part.

While Allison gave her attention to the list of clues, Jay stole a few moments to observe her. He liked her height; she reached up to his chin, a good fit to his six-foot-two frame. He thought he saw a faint dusting of freckles across her nose, but in the dim light cast by the elegant lampposts, he couldn't be sure. He liked the idea of freckles; he wanted to get closer to be certain.

He loved her riot of curls; they caused his fingers to ache with the need to run though the cinnamon-colored tresses.

She glanced at him, a tiny smile playing on her lips. She'd finally started talking to him and seemed reasonably intelligent. Too bad she was off her rocker.

"I wonder who Paige has as 'suspects.'"

Her gaze became confused as she caught his expression. She stepped into the light and he confirmed that yes, light freckles did dance across her nose and flushed cheeks.

"What?" she asked.

I never knew freckles were so sexy. "Nothing." His stride lengthened. The sooner he got this over with, the better. He couldn't control his reaction to her, especially now that he knew she could accomplish more than a fish imitation. She was too potent, too sensual; he didn't trust that. He didn't like the feelings she brought out in him, the ones that caused him to ache with desire, the ones that demanded he get closer to her.

Perhaps if he got to know her better, it would nip his attraction to her in the bud. Nothing like an obnoxious personality to kill a man's libido. Hopefully she had one.

"So, Mrs. Talbot tells me you're a mystery writer." She stiffened instantly; he could tell she didn't appreciate him knowing what she did for a living. Maybe she got tired of talking about it. Perhaps she didn't enjoy much success.

Or perhaps she felt a bit embarrassed by her career choice. After all, writers didn't always get the respect they deserved. At least Jeff had told him that. He'd been a screenplay writer before he'd turned his hand to acting.

"It must be a great way to make a living," he continued, trying to show her he respected her job. She must be published; the way Mrs. Talbot had talked about her with reverence hinted at that. "Must pay well, right?"

The spark of anger that lit her face left him in no doubt that he'd royally messed up. Great. Why couldn't he at least have gotten an ounce of that charm his brother oozed so easily?

Obviously book writing didn't pay well for her. He should have kept his mouth shut. He'd seen her apartment. Its starkness should have given him a clue that her finances weren't in great shape.

"My income is none of your business, and neither is my writing. So why don't we concentrate on solving these clues, and then you can go back to writing parking tickets or whatever it is you do."

Parking tickets? His jaw tightened in outrage. Before coming to Spokane, he'd worked the vice squad, one of the most dangerous and stressful departments to which a cop could be assigned. He opened his mouth to let her know what he really thought about writers, but her animated, angry gaze sparked a surge of emotion in him, one he recognized as excitement. Sexual excitement.

No. Not now. The timing stunk for this. And not with Allison Leavitt, wacky mystery writer. No matter how much she tantalized him, what could she have in common with a cop?

Nothing. The blunt answer was nothing.

I don't need this, he moaned to himself. He didn't realize he'd spoken out loud until he heard Allison's indignant gasp.

"I don't know what that chip on your shoulder is all about, but that doesn't give you an excuse to be rude."

Jay narrowed his eyes; the back of his neck throbbed.

"Look, I didn't ask to join this 'manhunt.' Your friend practically begged me to help you. Then that miserable mutt! Never mind. Point is, I'm still here. I'm trying to be a good sport about all of this."

Her blue eyes flashed angrily. "That 'mutt,' as you call him, is a valuable champion. And I'm sorry, but this is how you're a good sport? I'd hate to see you when you're miserable!"

'Misery' didn't fit his present mood. He felt certain parts of him tightening as he gazed into those incredible blue eyes, intensified by her errant copper curls.

"I'm not miserable."

"Ha! If you're having fun, then I'm a monkey's maiden aunt!"

He smiled at the mental image her statement created. Allison's frown faded. "You should do that more often." Her voice poured like whisky over ice; its husky timbre caressed his skin.

He didn't understand. "Do what?"

"Smile like that. It's positively fatal."

His pulse leapt at her observation. "I'll remember that." Her eyes sparkled in the dim light; he found he couldn't break away, until a movement off to the side caught his eye.

Pivoting, he discovered Birdie Talbot standing in the shadows, the much-abused Ping clutched to her chest. The dog looked none the worse for wear, despite the punting incident.

Realizing that Jay had spotted her, Birdie glared at him, obviously having overheard his disparaging remarks regarding her pet. She walked toward them, Ping's bell jingling merrily.

Funny. He hadn't heard that bell earlier.

"Allison!" Birdie exclaimed. "Did you find all the clues? I can't believe I forgot all about your party. Sometimes I swear that I'm going to forget who I am someday." Birdie's hair, a fluff of orange curls that were teased and stiffly hair sprayed, didn't move in the soft breeze that ruffled her voluminous muumuu. She didn't give Jay a glance; apparently she still harbored a grudge over the punting incident. Ping, however, gazed malevolently at his 'attacker,' a silent snarl twisting his lips. Jay glared back, answering him sneer for snarl.

He hadn't meant to toss the pooch, but an animal having sex with his shin wasn't something he'd ever put up with. That miserable Ping hadn't been about to let go; what were his other choices? Shoot the mutt?

"Jay, stop that!" Allison's fervent whisper broke his reverie. His gaze moved to Birdie, who now matched her pet's glare. Obviously she'd read his thoughts.

Damn. Ticking off his landlady wasn't a smart move, and he'd obviously accomplished exactly that.

"I collected all of Paige's clues, Birdie," Allison said. "It's time to start the game." Placing her hands on Birdie's shoulders, Allison turned her around, steering her toward the door. She glanced back at Jay. With a nod and a warning glare, she conveyed both 'come on' and 'behave!' to him.

He didn't have to be told twice.

Chapter Five

Allison drew in a deep breath as she entered the rec room. This was supposed to relax her? Having Mr. Lack-of-Manners tagging along sucked all the fun out of the evening for her. But that smile—wow! It curled inside her stomach, traveling both downward and up like a shiver. Why did such a delicious package have to contain such a sour disposition? At least she'd gotten over her inability to speak around him; now she just wanted to ignore him.

His disagreeable personality could be her saving grace. His looks and smile had been irresistible to her until his attitude had reminded her why she didn't want a man in her life.

Besides, she had goals. Goals she'd meet soon; this next book, after royalties started pouring in, would provide more than enough to see her pet project come to fruition. Other people might have scoffed at her dream of funding a state-of-the-art spinal research center, but to Allison, it would be worth all the sacrifices she'd made to see it succeed. She owed that not only to herself, but to…

She pulled her thoughts away from the past. She needed to stay focused on her current goals—finishing her book and getting the clinic up and running. Getting sidetracked by a guy simply because he resembled her ideal man didn't fit her plans at all.

There were nearly a dozen people in the rec room. Paige smiled brightly at her as she filled her plate from a buffet of sandwich and salad fixings. Standing beside her were the newlyweds, John and Carla Stiles from 1E. Recently back from their honeymoon, the pair glowed with love for each other. Allison tamped down her envy long enough to compliment Carla on her lovely silk dress in green, her trademark color.

Next were the two roommates that lived next to Jay. Dan and Keith were, respectively, a playwright and actor. She didn't understand their confused glances toward Jay, who resolutely ignored them.

Charles and Heather Ashton, both realtors, and their teenaged daughter, Sandra, were happily picking through the salad. Sandra waved exuberantly at Allison. She smiled back with affection.

The woman standing next to them, however, was another story. Allison knew that Paige wouldn't have invited Taffy, but that never stopped the woman from doing whatever she wanted. She went wherever she thought men might be.

She'd definitely dressed to trap a man. Her platinum blonde curls were piled high on her head, pinned with diamond clips Allison was certain were genuine. A cotton-candy-pink knit top displayed her abundant breasts prominently. White shorts left nothing to the imagination; her feet were encased in glittering, plastic, high-heeled shoes. She always dressed way over the top, but men still made a beeline toward her. The ones that didn't—well, if she wanted them, they didn't stand a chance. And tonight, Taffy's smiles were aimed in one direction.

Taffy had Jay in her sights and obviously planned on making a clean kill.

Allison's jaw clenched as she tried to tell herself she didn't care; Taffy was more than welcome to him. But somehow the words rang false. Who was she kidding?

Not even Jay deserved Death by Taffy.

For years, Allison had watched Taffy play her game. She'd flatter and charm her 'victim,' pulling him willingly into her web, where she'd keep him for months until she'd used up all of him she could. Then she'd spit him out, leaving a mere husk of a man while she moved on to another, usually wealthier sucker.

She reminded Allison of a female Nick.

Taffy was the reason Pearce and Paige weren't together. Paige had gone to his place one day to find Taffy leaving—with only half her clothes on and a satisfied smile plastered on her face.

Allison had never challenged Taffy over a man. She didn't have the looks or guts to out-charm the other woman. This time, however, she couldn't let her get away with sucking the life out of another victim.

No, someone needed to stand up to Taffy the Terminator.

As she walked toward Jay, ready to battle, a thought formed: *Does that someone have to be me?*

Taffy didn't spare Allison a glance. Her world revolved around men; Allison didn't even figure in her universe. She reached Jay first and pulled no punches. Her eyes sought his out, her long eyelashes fluttered as a flirtatious smile graced her lips. Vivid green eyes that came from contact lenses traveled up and down his lithe form; her soft sigh told Allison she liked what she saw. As Jay returned the perusal, Allison halted. She was too late.

🐾 🐾 🐾

Jay watched the blonde with the extra cleavage coming his way. It didn't take a genius to figure out her identity. Pearce's description fit her exactly. His partner didn't talk much to him, but in a few terse sentences, he'd warned him about Taffy.

As she reached him, the woman's overly red lips parted suggestively. "You must be our new neighbor. You look very familiar. I could swear I know you from somewhere. I'm –"

Jay held up a hand. He'd heard this all before from people who'd seen Jeff on television and couldn't quite reconcile his resemblance. He saw that same confusion on the two guys he'd just met, Dan and Keith. They must have noticed his likeness to his increasingly famous twin.

"No, don't tell me. You're Taffy."

Her face lit with pleasure. "We've met before?"

A faint grin curled Jay's lips. For those who knew him, that humorless smile acted as a warning. Poor Taffy had no clue.

"No, we've never met." His smile vanished as if it had never existed. "Pearce told me about you. It's almost like I know you." His voice carried easily; all conversation about them died.

Taffy's smile disappeared; her voice faltered. "Pearce?"

"Yes. He told me you were rather taken with him. Wanted to get cozy with him, he said."

Taffy must have picked up on his mood; her expression became guarded. "What else did Pearce tell you?"

His mouth twitched lazily. "He's my partner. Partners talk." Okay, that was a stretch, considering Pearce's lack of acceptance of him, but Jay didn't dwell on it. "He told me how you made it clear that you'd love to go to dinner with him, and that afterwards you'd show him a good time. But not just any dinner, mind you. You only go first class."

Taffy smiled, once again laying on the charm. "Is there anything wrong with knowing what I'm worth?"

Jay shook his head slowly. "No, not at all. So tell me, Taffy, would you date a poor man?"

Her eyes hardened slightly; to most people it would have been undetectable, but Jay was trained to read subtle clues. "I wouldn't waste myself on a poor man."

"So his heart and love wouldn't be enough for you? You'd need his money and gifts as well?"

Taffy ran her hands seductively over her curvy body. Jay could imagine that gesture worked on most men. Luckily, he didn't fall into that category.

"Honey," she purred. "What you see takes a lot of maintenance. Why shouldn't I expect some help with its upkeep?"

"So what you're saying is that you need to be reimbursed before you'll share your...assets?"

Taffy's face flushed with shock and anger. "Are you calling me a hooker?"

Jay shrugged. "Not at all." He waited until the tension left her gaze before speaking again. "With a hooker, you know what the price is up front."

He watched his words find their target, then turned and walked away. His work was done; he'd exacted justice for Pearce, as a good partner should. Not that Pearce would appreciate it, but Jay didn't like women who used men. He'd been the victim of one recently. Any chance he had to stop one, he'd take it.

He'd fleetingly played with the idea of getting Taffy to confess she'd never gotten anywhere with Pearce. The intrusive thought that Allison might be the object of Pearce's affections had stopped him. He didn't like the idea of her with another man.

He didn't want her for himself; he felt too raw after the disaster his life had become in L.A. One casual affair, one woman's lies and he'd been sent out of town like an out-of-control teenager to military camp. He was thirty-five, not seventeen. He'd deserved better, but his paranoid, politically-minded boss hadn't wanted to wait for the scandal to die down. Instead he'd placed Jay securely out of the way.

Jay frowned. Life hadn't been easy lately. He let his gaze flicker to Allison's addictive features.

At least it could turn out to be interesting.

🐈 🐈 🐈

Allison watched the scene before her, incredulous. Taffy, obviously disbelieving what she'd heard, beat a hasty retreat from the rec room and Allison gaped after her. That was it? That was Death-by-Taffy versus Jay-the-Socially-Inept? Wow. She could declare it no contest.

She vowed to never get the man angry with her.

"Come on, Al!" Paige approached at a fast clip. "Display your clues. I want to see if you found them all so we can get the game under way." Paige moved closer, whispering in her ear. "And wasn't the floor show worth it?"

Allison flashed her a reproving look. "I feel sorry for Taffy. Nobody deserves to be put down like that." One glance at Paige's disbelieving stare cracked Allison's self-control. She giggled. "Oh, yeah, it was good."

Paige cackled. "It's like my greatest fantasy come true." Her eyes gleamed with satisfaction. "So are you enjoying yourself?"

Paige's words held an unspoken question: was Allison clicking with Jay?

Allison grimaced. She doubted anyone could 'click' with that man. He held himself apart from everyone, remaining aloof and cool.

"He's hard to get to know. I'm not sure it's worth the effort." What could they have in common? True, she wrote about a cop, but that didn't help her understand Jay Cantrall. Ben Stark also kept himself distant, but he'd learned to open up to those he loved. It was much easier on paper to figure out a man's way of thinking than it would be in real life.

Not that she wanted to, she reminded herself. Nope.

"Not worth the effort? Al, how can you say that? That package is so...scrumptious! He looks like a movie star. Are you dead below the neck? You've had a parade of gorgeous men pass through that apartment next door to you, and not once did I see you take a second look... until now."

Allison turned her startled gaze to her friend. Could Paige be right? Was she so turned off of guys that she never bothered to even look? It had been over two years since her last date, she realized. She thought about all the men who'd lived in Jay's apartment before him, and not one stood out to her, not even Pearce, who'd caused Paige to fall deep and hard.

Birdie moved tenants in and out of 1A so frequently that everyone surmised she had some sort of hang-up over that apartment. Every few months, Birdie would find an excuse to relocate the tenant. On one occasion, the floors needed refinishing; another time all the windows were replaced, and once she swore she smelled smoke and had all the wiring updated. The reasons became more elaborate, but with the same result: a revolving door existed on the apartment next to Allison.

Allison smiled at the thought of Birdie's antics. She loved Birdie Talbot, who'd rescued her when her life had spiraled out of control. Allison had left those wild days behind her. She'd learned the hard way to play it safe, to take no risks.

Paige nudged her again. "Clues, girl, clues!"

Allison pulled the various objects out of her canvas bag, spreading them on the table, except for the Hot Wheels car, which Jay had. He'd been the one to retrieve that clue in order to hurry up the game.

Finding him with her eyes in the large room, she crossed to him, intent on retrieving it.

She braced herself for that jolt of electricity that seemed to happen whenever she shared space with Jay. Sure enough, it started in the pit of her stomach and ricocheted right through her. Hopefully, her face didn't show the turmoil he caused inside of her.

He leaned against the wall, separate from everyone. During her conversation with Paige, she'd noticed a couple of people attempting to talk to him, but they had soon scurried away.

Allison almost felt sorry for him, but his brusque treatment of her left her very little room to feel sympathy. Apparently police work didn't teach social manners.

"Jay." His eyes flicked to her; for an instance, she could see welcome in their depths, then his expression became shuttered. Her hand reached out to him in compassion, but she stopped herself. She'd realized that he didn't like being touched. Apparently he didn't want his space invaded.

"Could I have the car, please?" Straightening up, he fished in his pocket for a moment. Pulling his hand out, he revealed a small green metal car.

"Oh, my gosh!" With stunned reverence, Allison reached for the tiny car. "It's a redline 1967 Barracuda! I've been wanting one for ages!" Eyes dancing with delight, she grinned at Jay. "It's in much better shape than most I've seen. These are usually in 'played in' condition. The redlines are wonderful!" With her index finger, she indicated the tiny red circles painted on each miniature tire. Flipping the car over, she smiled in delight. "It's an original! Oh, where's Paige?"

She looked around the room and quickly found her talking to Don. Paige grinned and wiggled her fingers at Allison. When Allison's gaze flitted back to Jay, she caught his amused grin.

"What?" She half-laughed in confusion. Jay's smile widened, and she nearly jumped at the shivers of delight that coursed through her. Why did he have such an effect on her?

"You're like a kid at Christmas, and all over a tiny chunk of green metal. Why do these things fascinate you?"

She held the little car reverently. "I don't know. Maybe it's memories of playing with these with my brother when we were small. He still lives in California, with his wife and two boys. They always know what Auntie Al is giving them—Hot Wheels!" She laughed in delight at the memories. "They love them almost as much as I do. They demand two of each—one to leave in the package and one to play with."

Jay took the little car from her and studied it. "How much is something like this worth?"

Allison shrugged, feeling a bit disappointed in him. First, he'd questioned her income, now he seemed too curious about the price of this little car. She sensed an obsession with money. "About twenty dollars, I think, but that's not the real value. It's the enjoyment it brings people."

Jay tossed it back. "It's only a chunk of metal, Allison."

His reply dampened her happiness. "Jay, some things mean more to people than their face value. Like Ping, for example. To us, he's just a dog, but to Birdie, he's her best friend."

His lip curled in derision. "She must be pretty desperate for attention, then. That little mutt is the ugliest thing I've ever seen. Can't she make any human friends?"

His words, said into a momentary silence, carried too far. Birdie stiffened and turned toward them. Outrage tightened her features as she crossed the room.

Allison nodded to a point beyond Jay's shoulder. "Ask her yourself. She's right behind you." At this rate, she thought silently to herself, apartment 1A would soon be available.

🐈 🐈 🐈

Jay froze as a sinking feeling rushed through him. Closing his eyes with a sigh, he thought briefly about how to extract himself from this. Nothing came to mind. With an air of defeat, he turned to face his landlady. He could tell she'd heard him by her stiff posture and angry face. Even the little rat-dog looked put out as he sat regally in her arms.

The lease he'd signed had a clause, stating that either party could end it after a month. At this rate, he'd only have three weeks to find another place. Jay didn't relish that task at all. He gave his full attention to Mrs. Talbot, trying his best to smile apologetically. Apparently it fell far short.

Her eyes remained hard as nails; gone was the vacantly pleasant look she usually wore. She gazed at him as if he were an insect she wanted to squash. Ping curled one lip to show his dislike, followed by a widely spraying sneeze. Jay forced himself to curb his reaction as the damp mist settled on his skin, but his eyes shot daggers at the mutt.

"It might be time to remodel bathrooms, Allison," Birdie said, her eyes never leaving Jay. "I know just where to start."

Chapter Six

Allison could feel the anger boiling off of Jay. If he were anyone else, she'd conclude that he'd gotten what he deserved. But there was something about Jay that tugged at her senses; she couldn't quite dismiss him as an insensitive jerk.

Yet.

"Birdie, the bathrooms are fine, especially in Jay's apartment," she said. "You had it done only two years ago, remember? Why don't we play Paige's game and forget about this silliness."

Birdie glared at Jay for another moment, then, with a sharp nod, she left to plop down on a couch.

Allison turned to Jay. "You really need to watch what you say around Birdie. She loves that dog; he's like a child to her. Would you put up with anyone talking badly about your child?"

Jay shrugged. "I don't have children, and if mine misbehaved as badly as that one did, I don't think I'd attack the victim of my child's crimes."

Allison snorted. "You think you're a victim of a ten pound dog? That's a pretty weak stretch there, Officer."

"Detective," Jay corrected.

"Fine, *Detective*. Shall we solve the murder?" She smiled, but knew that it didn't reach her eyes.

The game commenced. Each 'suspect' concealed a hint about the clues; Allison merely needed to match the 'suspect' to the clue they had information about to get the hint.

Not an easy task.

As she surveyed the clues, the others, seated around the room on oversized couches, gave their 'motives' for wanting her 'dead.' Poor Birdie struggled with that concept. She paused for a moment, then declared, "Oh, Allison, I'd never want to hurt you!"

Laughing, Allison replied, "Birdie, I know that! This is just for the game."

"Oh, the game!" Frowning, Birdie thought for several moments, then smiled brilliantly. "You skinny-dip after midnight, and I've had to threaten all the male tenants here not to watch! I'm tired of that! How's that?" She beamed with delight first at Paige, who choked with laughter, then at Allison.

Allison felt her cheeks flaming, and she wanted to sink into the floor. She'd always thought that everyone was asleep on the rare occasions she'd skinny-dipped, but now she knew better. It was a remnant of her thrill-seeking days; she craved that tiny little glimpse of physical freedom.

Burying her face in her hands, she weathered the laughter. Finally, she dared a peek to find Jay gazing at her, his mouth twitching suspiciously.

"You know, I can see that as being a great motive to 'knock you off' for the women in here," he said. "It'll make narrowing down the list difficult."

The room burst into laughter yet again. Her face back in her hands, Allison mumbled, "Fine time for you to develop a sense of humor, Detective."

She felt a whisper of breath on her ear.

"I heard that."

Stacia Wolf

Groaning yet again, Allison lifted her head and glared at him. His mischievous little grin caused her pulse to race.

If he did that more often, she'd be a goner. That tiny glimpse of humor did wonders to his face, softening the hard planes and bringing a glimmer to his eyes that made her imagine them dancing with passion for her.

Stop it, She tore her gaze away from him, staring instead at the clues, even though they no longer held any interest for her. Only Jay did. She glanced at him just as he spoke to the room.

"Okay, let's move on." Jay's eyes landed on the newlyweds. "How about you two? What's your motive for this 'murder?'"

John smiled at Allison. "Oh, mine's the usual. She always takes the best parking spot."

Carla laughed at her husband's answer. "Mine's much more basic than that. She looks better in a bikini than I do."

Laughter erupted again at Carla's answer. Allison wondered if her face would be permanently scalded red as Jay's gaze moved over her appraisingly. Her loose tank top and shorts were definitely not figure flattering, and compared to Taffy's heart-pounding outfit, Allison felt downright dowdy. But Jay's expression showed loud and clear that he liked what he saw.

Maybe he had some redeeming value after all.

Maybe you could indulge…

Images of her and Jay entangled in her sheets invaded her thoughts. The fantasy was so clear and tantalizing that she felt her face flame again. Jay's easy grin told her that luckily, he couldn't read her mind. She'd die of embarrassment if he could.

They finished going around the room, and she was no closer to figuring out who was the 'killer' than she'd been before. Of course, she knew the motives were strictly for fun; it was Paige's own version of 'Celebrity Roast.'

Allison studied the clues again. A salt shaker, a red silk orchid, a jar of what looked like small pickled fish, a pink baby bootie, the green Hot Wheel and a red, wax candle in the shape of the number 'two.' None of them made any sense.

"Okay, Sandra." She smiled at the teenager. "Is your clue red?"

Sandra giggled. "Almost," she replied.

"Sandra!" Paige scolded. "Yes or no answers only!" Her admonition was softened by a fond smile.

Unrepentant, the girl grinned. "Sorry."

"Pink bootie!" Allison crowed. "Now tell me your clue!"

Sandra giggled again. "It's one word, Al. Sex!"

Sandra's mother groaned. "Paige, you had to give her *that* clue?"

Paige shrugged, her mouth twitching. "About time she learned to say the word." She laughed at Heather's mock glare.

"Gender. The killer is a woman." Jay's terse words cut through the banter.

Paige nodded. "Very good, Detective. But who?" When he didn't reply, she grinned. "Not that easy, huh?"

His smile was enigmatic. "We'll see."

Allison forced her mind away from Jay's addictive half-smile back to the clues. Okay, that left the fish, red flower, candle, salt shaker and car. Allison frowned for a moment, wondering what to ask next. Inspiration struck her.

"Heather, is your clue consumable? Like edible or if used, would be used up?"

Paige groaned. "I don't believe you!"

Jay lifted his brows, one corner twitching in amusement. Allison's senses jumped at the sight; why did he have to be so sexy?

"It's a yes or no question," he said. "Fits your rules."

Heather waited for a nod from Paige, and then replied, "No, it's not." That left Allison two choices. The flower or the car.

"Is it the car?"

Paige's groan was her answer. Chortling at her good fortune, Allison jiggled up and down on the balls of her feet.

"Okay, give me my clue!"

Heather extracted a paper from her pocket, and studying it for a moment, stated, "Handle."

"Handle?" That didn't make any sense to Allison; what did that have to do with the killer? She tried to think of other names for a handle, especially a car handle, but came up with knob or lever, which didn't help at all.

"Paige, your clues should actually make sense.

"I know who the killer is."

Jay's flat statement stole the air from her lungs. Turning toward him, she absorbed his confident yet reserved demeanor.

Paige snorted at his statement. "How could you have it already?"

Jay's face gave nothing away, yet something about the gleam in his eyes, the set of his strong jaw told Allison he'd discovered the answer.

"Go ahead, Jay," she said softly. "Tell us your reasoning."

His shrug was negligible. "Simple, really. The clues: the flower for a tropical destination, along with the salt indicating an ocean. The gender is female, which eliminates a few suspects. But the kicker is the green car."

"The car?"

He nodded slightly. "Once Heather gave her clue, it all fell into place." He picked up the toy, displaying it to the others. "I first thought Barracuda when I looked at this, but that's too precise. It's just a car. A green car." A corner of his mouth lifted. "Green, as in the killer's clothing color. Car, as in... Carla. Hence the 'handle' clue. Handle can also mean name."

All eyes swiveled to the newlyweds. Carla, her eyes widening, gazed at Jay. "Wow. You *are* good."

Allison could only stare. She didn't know her mouth hung open until Jay leaned toward her, whispering, "You're doing that fish thing again," then softly lifted her chin up.

Paige sighed. "So much for all my ingenious clues." She crossed her arms. "The salt was for the Pacific Ocean and for the margaritas Carla always makes. The orchid was for Hawaii, where they went for their honeymoon, and the candle stood for their apartment on the second floor."

"And the fish?"

"Oh, that one I know!" Birdie exclaimed. "The fish are exactly what they look like. They're red herring!"

Allison groaned. "Paige, that's really lame!"

Paige laughed with the others. "Hey, this was all for fun. I didn't expect Jay to be so clever, though, and solve it this quickly." Pushing herself off the couch, she said, "I think I'll grab a bit more to eat, then start cleaning up. I want to get up early and work on a new design." An interior designer, Paige created décor for businesses, both large and small.

Nodding, Jay stepped back. Allison, a great observer of human nature, saw the shutters falling quickly over his eyes. He was done. Time to retreat. She could see it in his face, in the way he stood. And she was perfectly willing to let him.

"I need to go as well. I've an early day tomorrow." Hands in pockets, Jay nodded at the room, then swiveled and headed out the door.

The instant the door shut behind him, the others turned to Allison. "Where did you dig him up?" Heather demanded.

Laughing, Allison said, "Don't look at me! Birdie rented him the apartment next door to me."

Birdie blinked. "Well, Pearce Randolph recommended him; how could I turn him down? Although I'm not sure he's the kind of person we want here. He doesn't like Ping!"

"Oh, how could anyone not like Ping?" Sandra asked, petting the cranky canine affectionately. Behind Birdie, Paige rolled her eyes. It was no secret, except to Birdie, that very few people enjoyed the company of the hairless canine.

Carla gave Birdie an affectionate squeeze. "He's probably not an animal person. I mean, he's pretty remote, isn't he? I tried talking to him and barely got a grunt in return. Too bad he's so gorgeous. It's such a waste."

"Woman, were you checking him out?" John spanned his hands around her waist and began to tickle her. Shrieking and laughing, Carla twisted away.

Chuckling at their antics, Heather said, "John, you can't blame her. That man has one fine backside." Slanting a look at her husband, she laughed when he glared at her.

"You keep an attitude like that, and I'll cut you off," Charles threatened his wife, a smile softening his words. Allison could see the love brimming between the two, even after almost twenty years of marriage. She admired that; she envied that.

Envied?

The thought stopped her for a moment; did she want what they had? No, of course not. Trying to find it was too much work, and involved way too many pitfalls along the way. Even if she found something worth hanging onto, could she be certain it was genuine? She thought of the soaring divorce rate and knew the answer to that one.

Her musings depressed her. Sometimes a solitary life became a burden. It would be nice to have someone to lean on in the tough times, and to crow with during the good ones.

She felt a warm hand on her arm, and turned to find Birdie smiling at her inquisitively, Ping propped comfortably on one arm. "Are you all right, dear?"

Allison smiled with deep affection. Years ago, when her life had gone tumbling down, she'd felt that same touch and heard the same words from this woman, and her life had turned around. She'd been buried in an envelope of pain and self-pity, and Birdie had pulled her loose from all that.

She covered Birdie's hand with her own. "I'm fine. A bit tired, I guess."

Birdie frowned. "You work too hard when you write. You need to pace yourself better. Oh!" Her fingers flew to her temple. "I just remembered something I found online today that I wanted to show you. I printed it out. Come on. We'll sneak over to my place and I'll get it for you. And I'm dying to know what's in that box I gave you earlier."

With all the activity, Allison hadn't opened the package yet. Birdie's enthusiasm was contagious, however, and curiosity suddenly won over exhaustion. "Sounds like fun. Let's go."

Giggling like two children, they snuck out, heading toward Birdie's apartment.

Chapter Seven

It didn't take long to find what Birdie was looking for: an article from a writer's magazine web site. Birdie wrote constantly. From time to time, she'd give Allison something to read, and Allison dreaded it. How could she tell her friend that her writing was awful? She tried to get her to sign up for writing classes, but so far Birdie had resisted, telling her that the teacher couldn't be half as helpful as Allison was, so why should she pay money for something she didn't need?

Birdie handed her the best-selling list, broken down by genre. There, at the top, Al Leavitt stood out.

"Oh, my gosh! I'm at the top?" Her last book, *Terminal Credit*, was about murders taking place at a long-running Broadway play. Released over a month ago, she'd never expected it to reach the top rung, a spot usually occupied by Robert B. Tyler, a long-standing icon in the murder-mystery ranks. Allison still waited with excitement for his latest releases, each guaranteed to be a page-turner.

"You've dethroned Robert Tyler!" Birdie grinned. "I'm so excited for you!"

Allison stared at the list. Her heart pounded at the reality of it: her last book had outsold Robert Tyler's! Nobody outsold Robert Tyler. But hers had.

"Wow," she breathed, eliciting a jiggling giggle from Birdie, who wrapped her arms about her as she bounced enthusiastically.

"I'm so proud of you! I knew you could do it!" She grabbed Allison's arm, pulling her out of her apartment. "Now let's go see what's in that package, shall we?"

They dashed in unladylike fashion next door to Allison's apartment. The box sitting near the computer carried her agent's address. Digging in the desk drawer, Allison found a box-cutter and slashed through the tape swiftly. The box revealed a large stack of paper. Allison stared at it in confusion. *What on earth…?* She didn't have anything with her agent right now that he'd be returning.

"Oh, my, it's a script!" Birdie said. "Allison, are they making a movie of one of your books?"

"I sold the movie rights to my first book a while ago. I'm supposed to get to read the first draft. Honestly, I'd almost forgotten about it." Most books that were sold for movies didn't make it to the big or small screen; Allison hadn't counted on it at all. But here was the script in her hands. She blinked away a tear. "I couldn't have done it without you, Birdie," she whispered.

"Of course you couldn't," Birdie replied, thumbing through the script. "Oh, dear, that sounded so arrogant, didn't it?"

Allison smiled. "No, it sounded honest." She'd been worse than down-and-out when she'd first met Birdie. She'd been lost and without a clue.

Her parents had been stuck in California after her father had undergone emergency heart surgery. Her brother had been trying to hold her father's dry-cleaning business together when Allison had been injured in a terrible climbing accident. She'd been all alone, first in a hospital, then in a rehab facility, with only sporadic visits from her mother.

Birdie had been a volunteer there, handing out books and cheer. She'd latched onto Allison and had never let go. For that, Allison would always be grateful. When she'd finally been discharged from full-time rehab, she'd come to live here.

There'd never been any question of that. Allison loved Spokane; L.A. contained all the things she hated about a big city: smog, traffic, confusion, and intolerance. Spokane, while about a half-million people big, still felt like a small town to her. In L.A., her family had never even known their neighbor's names. Here, she knew everybody.

After the accident, she'd been broken in spirit as well as body. While she'd physically healed, her mind hadn't fully let go of that day over seven years before. The horror of the accident would often surface: climbing that rock face, reaching the top, shouting in victory, then the screams from below. She'd looked down and seen a young boy, not more than thirteen, clinging to the rock, his body paralyzed with fear. The boy had climbed up almost forty feet before freezing; he was about fifty feet below her. He had no safety rope, and Allison was the only one hooked up to any climbing equipment. She was also the closest.

Another climber had handed her a spare belt, and she'd rappelled down to him. She'd talked to him, tried to calm him, to get him to let her hook the belt onto him so he could climb up or down, but his fear had overridden everything. He'd never climbed before and had only done so on a dare by his friends, who'd watched, horrified, from below. Then one of them, trying to make light of it, had said, "He can't climb as good as a girl. Now he has to be rescued by one."

The boy, reacting to the other's words and trying to save what little remained of his pride, had pushed Allison away, yelling that he could finish. But the shove had thrown him off-balance and he'd begun to slip. He'd screamed as he'd fallen. Somehow Allison was able to get hold of his arm. His weight had twisted her shoulder, but she'd held on, hauling the boy toward her. She couldn't get the belt on him now. All she'd been able to do was slowly descend, talking to him all the while, hoping her arm would hold up and that they'd make it down safely.

Her equipment, however, hadn't handled the stress; the harness gave way, and they'd fallen. They were still over twenty feet above the rocks.

Down, down, twisting; a silent scream on her lips. Impact. The helmet on her head split in two. Pain.

Allison didn't like to think about it. All that was gone now; she lived a much safer, risk-free life these days. Those types of things never happened in Allison Leavitt's world. They were relegated to the dim past. Once bitten, twice shy. That went for dangerous activities as well as men. Allison embraced that philosophy as her life's guide. The only risks she took these days dealt with her writing. That was all she needed.

Smiling widely at Birdie's exuberant face, Allison told herself that it *was* indeed all she needed.

Then why did she have to banish Jay's image from her mind?

"How's your project going?" Birdie asked.

"This next book should do it," Allison grinned her excitement. She'd planned this rehab center for years. With the income from some major investments she'd made, local agencies would run the program for underprivileged children who'd suffered spinal or head injuries and required extensive rehabilitation. The remodeling on the building would be finished soon. The documents outlining the legalities and the treatment available for the kids had been drawn up. Now all that remained was the health district's blessing and finalizing the staff. Allison hoped that by the first of the year, the center would be up and running.

She silently thanked Birdie for distracting her with talk of the center. She'd started wondering what it would be like to have someone in her life and had forgotten the more important things. Like the rehab center, her friends, her family, and staying free from entanglements. Especially ones that involved cranky cops like Jay Cantrall.

🐈 🐈 🐈

Jay accepted the coffee from his partner gratefully; the hot Styrofoam cup in his hands felt welcome. Even in early July, the Spokane morning air held a nip to it. Pearce sat on the bench beside him, holding his own cup. Inhaling the hot steam, Pearce sighed in delight.

"Man, that smells good. I hope this idiot shows up soon, so we can make an arrest and head back to the station."

Jay nodded in agreement as he took a sip. Stakeouts, and this one in particular, were definitely not his favorite part of police work. They'd been watching this location in downtown Spokane for nearly a week now and their target still hadn't shown. They were told he always frequented the same coffee shop, but so far, no show.

Jay's personal belief followed the lines of 'wild goose chase;' Pearce, however, believed his informant's tip. If it was right, this would be a big break in the car theft case that Jay had been sent to help resolve.

They'd chosen to watch the coffee house from across the street in Riverfront Park. A partially enclosed booth that served as a waiting area for the gondola ride afforded them a good view of the shop. It also gave them an advantage; the smoky glass couldn't be easily seen through from the outside, yet they could see out without difficulty.

Jay would have liked to try the gondola. It offered its passengers a bird's eye view of Spokane River's waterfalls. While the stakeout was happening, the ride had been shut down for 'service' to keep people away from Jay and Pearce, who posed as maintenance workers. Even if it was running, his discomfort with his new partner would have restrained him.

Pearce Randolph had yet to warm up to the thought of Jay as his partner. Jay could commiserate; the man hadn't been given a choice. Jay'd been transferred to Spokane in disgrace, and then tossed in Pearce's lap like a sack of dirty laundry nobody had wanted to deal with. Forget the fact that Jay was a good cop with a spotless record. Until now.

He shifted his mind on to other things, like getting along better with his new partner. Who knew how long this 'transfer' would last? He might as well make the best of it.

"I met your friend, Taffy, last night."

Pearce arched a brow. "Oh, yeah? Did she make a move?"

Jay's mouth twisted cynically. "Exactly like you said."

"And what did you do?"

Jay gave him a blow-by-blow of his exchange with Taffy. He didn't mention his motivation had been to bring down a bit on revenge on her for Pearce's sake. Although he knew it to be the right thing to do, Jay and Pearce weren't partners in the full sense of the word. Not yet. And probably never would be.

News of the reason for his transfer had preceded him. His fellow officers' showed an intense dislike of the disgraced 'pretty boy.' Pearce, now receiving a great deal of teasing over his new partner, had to be feeling a lot of resentment.

Right now, that emotion didn't show as Pearce smiled. "Man, wish I'd been there to see that. I still want to kick her for the trouble she caused me."

The 'trouble' Pearce referred to was the derailed romance he'd started with a resident of the apartments. He'd told Jay about it only in reference to Taffy. He'd never mentioned the name of the object of his affection, but Jay thought he knew: Allison. How could anyone resist those deep blue eyes and that riot of cinnamon curls? His stomach roiled at the idea of Pearce and Allison together. But for some reason, he had to know.

"I met Allison last night."

Pearce's intelligent gaze scanned Jay's face. "Did you now? What did you think of her?"

"Different. Her friend decided to cheer her up by 'killing' her."

Pearce snorted. "You must be talking about Paige. Harebrained ideas are her lot in life."

"You've got that right. She 'killed' her off with a red paintball. The fool landlady thought it was blood and dragged me into it to investigate her murder."

Pearce hooted. "Sounds like Birdie. Wonderful lady, but not all there."

"I think I figured out that much."

Pearce gazed back toward the coffee shop. "Sounds like I missed a fun time. Much better than the evening I spent with Lindsay." Lindsay was the woman his former love interest had fixed Pearce up with, that much Jay knew. Things weren't going well with her, despite the sunny picture Pearce painted for everyone else. Jay had figured that out by the myriad cell phone calls Pearce received from Lindsay in the last few days; most hadn't ended on a good note.

"Rough night?"

Pearce rolled his eyes. "Oh, 'rough' doesn't even cover it. But it's done. I told her last night I didn't want to see her anymore." Pearce's face twisted. "I don't think I'll be welcome at that restaurant for a while."

Jay whistled. "Must have been quite a scene."

Nodding, Pearce sipped the hot coffee. "Yeah. But it's over, so now I can see if I can get Paige back."

Jay's eyes snapped to his partner's face in shock. "Paige?"

"Yes, Paige. Who did you think?" Pearce guffawed. "You thought it might be Allison?"

"The idea had occurred to me."

"Don't get me wrong. Allison's a great person. But she's too smart for me. Plus, she acts like one of the guys. I don't think I've ever seen her in a dress. I prefer someone a bit more feminine. Like Paige. "

"Paige, huh? Pretty girl." Jay's mouth lifted. This was the closest he and Pearce had ever come to talking. The man actually seemed likable today.

"Wackier than a fruitcake. And more trouble than a pile of snarling dogs. But she suits me," He swirled his coffee. "And I want her back."

Jay stared out of the booth; through the trees, he could see the antique carrousel, now silent. Not much call for rides this time of the morning. "So what are you going to do about it?"

Pearce smiled a rueful grin, "Funny you should ask that."

🐾 🐾 🐾

"I don't see why you had to bring that mutt along," Paige groused. She sent a baleful glare Ping's way. The dog, decked out in a light purple sweater and little purple booties that accentuated his brown spots, remained unaffected by Paige's attitude as he trotted beside Allison.

"I've told you, Birdie felt that Ping was too upset from last night to be left alone. She had a meeting at the bank, and Ping's not exactly welcome there."

Paige grunted. "There's a shocker."

"Paige."

"What? I don't have to pretend to like the nasty little creature. And he sure doesn't look upset to me."

Allison's brows lifted. "I could have stayed home. I have a deadline looming ."

Paige waved away her words. "No, no, I need you here. Moral support and all that crap. I'll stop grousing about the mangy mutt." She stopped walking; Riverfront Park was now in view. "I don't know why Pearce called and asked to see me this morning. He sounded so intense, Al. I thought we were over all this serious stuff and were just friends."

Allison studied her friend. Impatience, fear and a remnant of the emotions she'd developed for Pearce lingered on her face. "Is that really what you want? Just friendship?"

Paige wrinkled her nose. "I thought I did. He hurt me badly over that Taffy thing. But I've missed him," She stared ahead at the park. "I'm not sure I want to do this."

"What do you think he wants to tell you?"

"I can only think of one thing," Her eyes glittered with tears. "He and Lindsay are getting married."

Allison's heart ached for her friend. "Oh, Paige."

Paige stepped off the curb, walking purposefully forward. "It's my fault, Al. He wanted to stay together but I couldn't stand the fact he'd cheated on me with that bimbo. So I went out of my way to prove to him he had no effect on me. And now he's getting married and I have to live with the consequences. So be it." Her chin lifted bravely as she walked; even her hair bounced in defiance.

"You don't know for sure what he's going to say."

"It can't be good, Al. Why else would he call me down here when he's working?"

She had a point. All of what Allison knew about stakeouts told her that personal fraternization was frowned upon.

"I'm sure his partner's with him. So I'll wait over here for you, okay?"

Paige nodded. "I'll be right back." She didn't question Allison's avoidance of Jay. For that, Allison felt grateful.

She sat down on a bench as she watched Paige cross over toward the gondola. Reaching down, she scratched Ping's chin. No. She wouldn't go anywhere. Not until Paige came back, hopefully with news other than an impending wedding.

🐾 🐾 🐾

"I see Paige." Jay kept his voice flat and impersonal. No need to let his partner know that he, too, was anxious for things to turn out right for Pearce. No need to mention that Paige looked so stressed that the weight of a feather might break her.

Pearce sucked in a deep breath, then let it out slowly. "Okay. Here I go." Standing up, he stepped out of the enclosure.

Several things happened at once. Paige stopped walking and stared at Pearce. He picked up his pace, his eyes only for Paige.

Their suspect appeared outside the coffee house, saw Pearce and apparently recognized him. He turned around and headed in the opposite direction.

"Damn," Surging out of the enclosure, Jay sprinted toward the fleeing man. "Pearce, he's on the run!"

His partner turned toward the coffee shop. Muttering an expletive, he ran after Jay.

Neither paid any attention to the insistent barking they heard.

🐾 🐾 🐾

"Hope she doesn't take too long, Ping," Allison told her sole companion as she gazed at the carrousel a few dozen yards from her. An antique, the Looff Carrousel had been built in 1909 as a present from the artist to his daughter. It had been carefully restored for the 1974 World Fair, which had been held in Spokane, and now enchanted thousands of children and adults alike every year.

If Ping listened to her, he gave no indication. Instead, he stared after Paige, his eyes never wavering.

As for Allison, she couldn't settle down. She'd dreamt of him last night. Of Jay—or Ben. She didn't know which, but he'd taken her in his arms and kissed her. Then he'd—

No, she wouldn't dwell on it. She felt so confused. Was she fascinated with Jay because of Ben Stark, or because of Jay himself? She needed time and distance to figure it out.

"I can't believe I let her talk me into this, pal. I don't need to run into Jay again, and he's probably only yards away. I don't know what it is about him."

A loud yip and a massive tug jerked Allison's attention back to Ping as he surged forward, jerking the leash from Allison's slack fingers. With speed reminiscent of a greyhound, Ping tore off across the park after his prey. It didn't take Allison two seconds to recognize who Ping was after: Jay.

Thanking fate that she'd worn her running shoes, Allison rushed after the little dog, hoping she could corral him before he got into trouble.

"Ping! No! Stop!"

🐾 🐾 🐾

Feet pounding, Jay could see the distance between himself and Alvin Morrow shrinking. Just a bit faster, just a little more, and he'd have him.

He could hear footsteps behind him, and shouting. Pearce had his backside; he didn't need to worry. The barking and ringing bell, growing louder and louder, didn't sink in.

Out of the corner of his eye, he caught a small purple streak heading his way; with a sinking feeling, he knew they were on a collision course.

Leaping and twisting, he attempted to sidestep it, but the streak didn't back off. He jerked sideways in midair to avoid it, but his landing was far from perfect. Landing on the side of his foot, he fell, his knee impacting with a sickening thud on the hard surface. Rolling his arms up to protect his head, Jay grunted in pain as his elbows smacked the pavement.

He felt a stinging nip on his arm as insistent yapping reverberated in his ears. He slapped at the air as he felt another nip. Sitting up, he recognized his miniature attacker—Ping!

The thud of footsteps approached, then he heard Pearce. "Jay, you all right?"

Considering the throbbing in his right knee, Jay could tell the answer would be no.

"I think," he panted, gripping his injured limb with one arm while fighting off his assailant with the other, "That I'm really starting to hate this dog."

Chapter Eight

"Excuse me, could you tell me where to find Mr. Cantrall?"

"Al! Over here!" At Pearce's voice, Allison turned away from the nurses' desk and found him standing a few yards away. She smiled at the nurse and then walked over to him.

She'd stopped to drop Ping off at Birdie's place, with a note explaining that someone had been hurt and she needed to check on him. She'd tell Birdie later that poor Ping had once again been involved in an altercation with Jay. After the punting incident, Birdie didn't quite see Jay in a favorable light.

Never mind that Allison had been negligent in letting Ping get loose in the first place, and that the dog had put himself in danger. Birdie wouldn't think about that. Instead, she'd focus on the fact that Jay had upset poor Ping.

And Jay would be asked to move.

For some reason, Allison didn't like that idea. He might be unfriendly, disagreeable and generally not her type, but he couldn't be all bad, could he? On the surface, he wasn't much different from the way she'd written Ben Stark: remote, self-contained, strong, stoic, mostly silent, except to his partner, Emily. Yet inside, out of the sight of human eyes, he loved; he laughed; he burned; he ached.

She knew what churned inside the mind of Ben Stark. After all, she'd invented him and populated his psyche with her ideas.

She didn't have a clue as to what lurked behind Jay Cantrall's eyes.

"How is he?"

Pearce shrugged, a familiar male gesture that showed both uncertainty and lack of control over a situation. "Doctor says he's out of commission for a few weeks at least. He has some micro tears to his tendons by the knee, and the kneecap area is badly bruised. He recommended some physical therapy. Poor guy's going to be wearing a brace for a while."

Allison shuddered. The blame resided solidly on her shoulders. If she'd been paying more attention to Ping instead of musing over Jay, this would never have happened.

Pearce placed an arm around her shoulders. "Al, it's not your fault. That little monster's uncontrollable. You did your best. Besides, Jay should've been able to jump over him, but I guess they don't give L.A. cops 'Animal Avoidance 101' like they do us more rural guys."

Allison attempted a smile at Pearce's lame joke, but inside her stomach churned. Her negligent behavior had injured a police officer, for heaven's sake! And allowed a probably hardened criminal to escape. How could she ever make up for that? The memory of Jay lying on the ground, jaw clenched against the pain, tore through her yet again.

"I couldn't control a ten pound dog, Pearce. He was on a leash. How hard is it to hold a leash?" She glanced toward the closed doors of the exam area. "I need to apologize to him, see if there's anything I can do."

Glancing at his watch, Pearce cocked his head slightly. "Well, if you're hanging around, I might as well get back to work and fill out all the paperwork waiting for me. I'll have to explain why I lost yet another partner." Pearce's last three partners hadn't lasted long with him. One had succumbed to marriage and a new bride who didn't want her husband in any danger. He'd transferred to a desk job. Another partner, a woman, became a newlywed and a first-time mom, and the third had become victim to mononucleosis. It would be at least another month before he'd return to work.

And now Jay.

"I guess if a cop wants some time off, or a different job, you're the man to help them," she said.

Pearce laughed. "You need to save your funnies for your books. So you can take him home for me?"

Panic flared. She couldn't be stuck in a car with Jay! Not with that disagreeable, obnoxious man! Pain could only make his attitude worse, and she knew she didn't want to see that.

"You're not coming back?" She barely noted that her voice squeaked in panic. "Don't you have some sort of partnership obligation to take care of him or something? Isn't that part of the unwritten code?"

Pearce laughed. "Good one, Al. An unwritten 'baby-sit your partner' rule. I like that," As he spoke, he moved closer to the exit. "I'm sure the two of you'll be fine. Tell Jay to call me with an update. Talk to you later." With a hurried wave, Pearce made his escape.

"Drat," Allison muttered. She didn't have time for this. Or the stomach. She needed to work on her book and read the screenplay. The last thing she wanted was Jay Cantrall as an anchor around her neck.

Sighing, she returned to the desk, asking if she could see her unwanted charge. Might as well make the best of it, she decided. After all, it was her fault. Just because she disliked him and he set her nerves on edge—well, she'd have to grit her teeth and live with it, wouldn't she?

🐈 🐈 🐈

"Ouch! Damn! Can't you miss a few bumps?" Even with the seat scooted all the way back in Allison's small, older-model Mazda Miata, Jay's knee still bent at an uncomfortable angle. He'd had to remove the knee brace the hospital had given him just to fit in this tiny trap of a car. He could feel each and every little dip in the road; the jolts traveled up his leg, creating shards of agony.

Allison's mouth tightened as she spared him a glance. "I'm sorry, but I'm crawling right now as it is. I wouldn't be surprised if we get a ticket for obstructing traffic flow."

Jay's eyes swept over the speedometer. She was right; they were traveling at a pace that was well under the posted speed limit. He thought longingly of the police-issued car that Pearce had taken with him. The back seat was wide and would have given him a lot of stretching room. Yet another black mark against his botched partnership.

His entire Spokane experience had left him with a bad taste in his mouth. Now this—this canine-caused catastrophe—had soured him totally on his enforced exile. The fact that Pearce left him in the care of the woman who'd caused his literal downfall was the final straw.

He'd call his boss and demand his return. Surely he'd simmered down by now.

The feeling of horror that had swamped him when the scandal had broken came back to him again. He'd hated being hounded by the press. The assistant DA's impending marital break-up involved more than just Jay; his wife had apparently slept with several prominent individuals on her way to divorce court. Having Jeff Cantrall, the TV star, as his twin brother had only made Jay more newsworthy than the situation had merited.

"Argh!" Another bump rocked all thoughts from his head as Allison apologized profusely. He closed his eyes to fight the nausea that twisted his gut.

No, this transfer definitely sucked. His entire life sucked. The only bright spot was the fact that his current tormentor sported the most beautiful blue eyes and enticing copper curls he'd ever seen.

🐎 🐎 🐎

Shoving a lock of hair behind her ear as she waited for her computer to boot up, Allison grumbled softly under her breath. She'd gotten nothing done all day. After depositing Jay in his bed, she'd hurried home just in time to receive a phone call from Paige, who could do nothing but talk about Pearce. Allison could hear the censure in her voice that said 'it's your fault we didn't get to talk—yours and Ping's!' But she didn't take the bait.

It took Allison nearly an hour to convince Paige to give Pearce a call. Not that Paige would do it. For all her bravado, she still suffered horribly from cowardice when it came to men.

Allison congratulated herself that her personal life wasn't as rife with stress as Paige's. Of course, technically, she didn't have a 'personal' life. But still, she had to admit loneliness clouded her existence lately. She also acknowledged that it was becoming harder and harder to shake off. But she wouldn't let it get her down.

She checked her e-mail, sent a swift reply off to a message from her father, and laughed at a photo of her nephews mugging for the camera in front of a display of her books at a California mall. There were a few other messages, but none that required her attention. Nothing that would quell her restlessness.

In previous years, this type of edginess would signal the need for an adrenaline rush, such as mountain climbing, parachuting or white-water rafting. But Allison had learned what trouble risk-taking could cause, and she'd mended her ways. Until last night, she'd combated it with a good jog in the park or a nude swim in the complex's swimming pool.

Her face burned as she remembered Birdie's declaration to the room about her obviously not-so-secret skinny-dipping. Well, that wouldn't happen again. Nope, done with burning off stress in that fashion. She'd have to find another way to relax.

Loud thumping emanated from her bedroom. Startled, her fingers tripped over the keys, producing gibberish on the screen. She rushed to the bedroom, expecting to find a collapsed shelf or some other unwanted damage. Instead, the room looked exactly the same as it had this morning.

Then what had made such a racket?

The wall reverberated with loud banging again, and she realized what caused it. Jay Cantrall, stuck in his bed next door, wanted her attention.

"Honestly," she muttered as she headed for the door. "Hasn't the man ever heard of the telephone?"

She didn't bother knocking on his door, having deliberately left it unlocked earlier. She knew that he'd need something sooner or later, and darned if she'd bother Birdie to let her in, or stand there cooling her heels while she waited for him to try and get to the door.

She swept through his apartment, still bothered by the lack of furniture or any personal touches that could help her decipher the man who lived there. All that occupied his living room was a couch, a wooden chair and a large television. Boxes were piled up in the dining room. Their small number told Allison one of two things: either he traveled lightly through life or he wasn't planning on staying. Or maybe, she mused, it was a combination of both.

"Allison, is that you?" Jay's voice sounded tired, and she recognized the pain underlying it.

"Yes, I'm here. And could you please call when you want my attention? You came damned close to rattling things off the wall." Entering the bedroom, she concluded that his appearance mirrored his voice. There were dark circles under his eyes; his lips were pulled taut. But none of that diminished his attractiveness; even the stubble on his chin, a shade darker than his sleep-mussed hair, added an air of danger to him. To a former adrenaline junkie like Allison, Jay looked like a man who could twang her heartstrings.

But she'd had all her shots and she'd swear by her immunity. Yes, no problem. Jay Cantrall couldn't affect her.

Until his eyes caught hers, that is, and she could see his relief at her arrival. Her traitorous heart went pitter-patter at his welcoming smile.

But that brief glimpse of humanity faded swiftly, to be replaced with that remote look she'd become familiar with in such a short time. She didn't like him, she reminded herself. His attitude stank. Ping didn't like him; weren't dogs a great judge of character? That should give her a clue to avoid the man...except his particular shade of gray eyes did something to her insides.

"I would call, but I don't have your number." He frowned his impatience, but even that didn't calm down her fluttering nerves.

"I put it on a sticky note by your phone."

"I didn't see one."

His shortness with her brought out a frown of her own. "I know I put it there. I—oh, there it is, on the floor." Bending down at the waist, she retrieved the errant note and placed it once again on Jay's rickety nightstand. Glancing at him, she found him staring up at the ceiling. "There you go. So, what do you need?" She tried to keep her impatience out of her voice; really, she did. But there were too many things to do, and not enough time to do them.

Stop it, she chided herself. She couldn't blame Jay for his predicament. If she'd paid more attention to little Ping, this wouldn't have happened and she wouldn't be stuck babysitting him. But it had happened and it was her responsibility to make it up to him. Somehow.

"I wanted to know if I could take another painkiller. I don't remember what time I took the one you gave me." His eyes closed, emphasizing his battle with the pain. Sympathy softened Allison. Glancing at her watch, she calculated the time and determined he could have another pill.

"Of course. They're in the bathroom. I'll get them for you."

"Don't bother. I have them." He displayed the bottle in his hand. "I didn't want to take them too soon, and I slept for a while. Wasn't sure how much time had passed."

No wonder he looked so tired; he'd retrieved the pills himself. She knew quite well that after an impact injury, a person's energy level bottomed out.

"Let me get you some water, then." She didn't give him a chance to turn down her offer. She filled a cup with cool water and set it on the nightstand. He fumbled with the pill bottle; from his supine position it was beating him soundly. Allison gripped her hands behind her back, fighting the impulse to rip the bottle away from him and open it herself.

With a growl of anger, Jay gave it a strong twist and the top flew off with a vengeance. Pills scattered over the bed and wooden floor.

"Damn!" Jay tried to sit up, but stopped abruptly with a sharp intake of breath.

"Lie down," she said. "I'll pick them up. Here." She put a pill in one of his hands and placed the water glass in the other. "Take that, let me clean this up and I'll get out of here so you can cuss to your heart's content."

She scooped up the pills off the bed, counting as she went. Then, on her hands and knees, she found all the other missing tablets. With a exultant 'yes!' she leaned her elbows against the mattress and smiled as she poured the pills from her hand back into the bottle.

"Allison..." Jay's hoarse voice jerked her gaze to him. A pulse throbbed in his tightened jaw; she could feel his desire for her, tangible in the air. His eyes were fastened on her plain, white, sleeveless sweater; with a startled downwards glance, she realized that the sweater gapped revealingly away from her, allowing him an unfettered view down to her waist. Her lacy ivory bra didn't exactly leave much to the imagination.

Heat suffused her face as she scrambled onto her feet. "I...I've got to go." She twisted the pill lid back on and slammed the bottle onto the night stand. Without a backward glance, she fled, humiliation speeding her feet. Once she reached home, she knew one thing—that sweater would be heading into the trash!

Chapter Nine

At the sound of Allison's retreating footsteps, Jay fell back against his pillows, the breath he'd held hissing through his lips. Damn, didn't the woman know how incredibly sexy she was? First, she crawled around the floor with her shapely fanny up in the air; those shorts that seemed so loose when she stood upright definitely hid nothing when stretched across that delectable backside. Then she'd leaned on the bed…

He could still see the curves of her breasts cupped so enticingly by that tiny scrap of lace as she'd leaned toward him, the triumphant smile on her lips so tempting that he'd felt his groin tighten and flame in response. One more instant in her company and he would have forgotten his injuries and his hatred of all women and kissed her senseless.

He closed his eyes, intent on purging her image from his mind. Instead, he succumbed to the fatigue that ached from his bones and fell into a deep sleep.

An insistent clicking roused him hours later; he knew without opening his eyes that Allison wasn't there. He didn't sense her; he didn't smell that spicy, warm scent that belonged uniquely to Allison. It took him a few moments to recognize the metallic sound.

Knitting needles. He remembered his grandmother, decades ago, sitting by him as he napped. The click of those needles had comforted him then, a clear signal that she was near.

It irritated him now. Because he was tired. And because they meant that Allison had fled. She didn't seem the knitting type; it could only be his landlady. In fact, he could smell that cloying, overpowering floral perfume of hers.

He didn't want her here. He wanted Allison. He wanted to see her, to try and figure out what it was about her that drove him so crazy.

No, he *needed* to see her.

Damn. Not the best situation for him. He held no attraction for her; that he knew. What could a beautiful but insane writer see in a crusty and banished cop?

That answer hadn't changed from before—nothing.

Opening his eyes to his current reality, he met Birdie Talbot's ice-cold gaze. She surveyed him with an air of disdain from a wooden chair pulled up next to the bed. Jay glanced around the room as the tiny Ping-bites on his hand began to throb.

"He's not here," she informed him coolly. "He finds being around you traumatizing."

"I know the feeling," Jay muttered, not caring if Birdie heard him or not. Her glare made it clear she had.

"Where's Allison?"

"She had a meeting. She'll be back soon."

"A meeting? Does she do something else for money besides writing?" He'd thought she concentrated solely on that. Maybe she had a part-time job to support herself.

"She does fine with her writing." Birdie clicked her needles again, a bit louder than Jay felt was necessary to pull and twist that yarn into what looked like a dog sweater. An ugly, garish dog sweater of pink, green and orange stripes. Couldn't the woman at least pick out matching colors for the poor pooch?

"Are you ready for a painkiller? Allison said you'd need one, which is why she asked me to sit with you, since you don't have my number and she wouldn't be home."

Jay lay back in bed. "I don't need a babysitter." His eyes closed without his agreement.

"No, you need a session with Miss Manners," Birdie said.

"What?" Had he heard her right? He snapped his gaze onto her face, trying to read her, but she gave nothing away.

"Never mind. Are you hungry? I can fix you some soup."

The single sheet that covered him stuck to his skin already from the muggy heat. "I hurt my knee. My stomach's fine."

Birdie snapped her needles together and stood up, setting them on the seat as she gathered up her yarn. "I'll take that as a no, you're not hungry. I see you're all right. Allison can check on you when she gets back."

Damn, all he could do lately was piss women off. "Look, I'm sorry—"

"Birdie." A hushed voice pulled his attention away from his landlady in time to see Allison peek into the bedroom.

She wore her typical tank top and shorts, but the top, a soft gray color with a Mariners logo on it, molded to her lush curves enticingly. She must have changed from the sweater, he mused, over embarrassment of 'flashing' him. But this one, demanding that his eyes soak in every tasty inch of her, became more than he could bear. He tore his gaze away, focusing instead on a slim cobweb hanging in the corner.

"Oh, you're awake," she said, stopping in the doorway.

"Yes, he is, and unfortunately, sleep didn't mellow him," Birdie said. "I'm going back to my apartment and check on Ping. Poor thing's been shaking all day." Picking up a bag brimming with yarn, Birdie Talbot huffed out of Jay's bedroom, followed by a firm slam of the front door closing.

"Wow." Allison's sigh dragged his gaze back to her. "You riled her up."

Jay closed his eyes, futilely trying to get his roiling blood pressure under control. Allison in tight shorts and top could cause any man heart failure, he decided. He definitely suffered from palpitations just from looking at her.

What was wrong with him? He never reacted to any woman the way he had with Allison. But something about her—her smile, her personality—pulled at his very soul.

It bothered the hell out of him.

But hell suddenly got hotter when he felt the bed sag beside him. Her body heat pervaded his senses; she smelled of raspberries and sunshine and woman. He stifled a moan, but he must have grimaced.

"You're in pain." Allison's cool hand touched his forehead. The contact sent shockwaves of desire through him. His breath charred his throat as it escaped. His hand jerked up to cover hers, intending to pull it away. He couldn't take anymore.

But her fingers fit against his like they were meant to be there. Her smooth, petal-soft skin became an instant addiction.

Boldness filled him, something he usually didn't experience with a woman. In the past, he'd bide his time, wait a while until he could feel out a woman's motives. But with Allison, he felt himself pulled into her, could sense how without deception she was. Her very lack of airs added to her sensuality. Almost without thought, he let his thumb curve around her palm, taking control of the moment.

He slid her hand down his cheek, settling it against his lips. Without thought, he tasted her warm, smooth flesh, relishing in his effect on her when her fingers tweaked in reaction. But she didn't pull away. He took that as encouragement and pulled one succulent fingertip into his mouth.

Her gasp sent shivers through his groin. Blood rushed downward, filling him with decadent thoughts about Allison and her soft, sweet curves.

The pain in his knee, the fuzziness in his head, melted away at the thought of touching her further, of exploring this strange connection he felt with her.

She tried to pull her hand free, but he held her firmly. Stealing a glance at her, he saw her eyelids flutter shut, then open partially to show her eyes rolling upwards in rapt pleasure. He'd never seen anything sexier, more enticing, more fulfilling.

How much better would kissing her mouth be? He had to find out.

He moved his lips to the inside of her wrist, loving the slightly salty, yet sweet, taste of her skin. She felt so soft, like smooth silk. He nibbled slightly and felt her pulse leap beneath his mouth. Upwards, onward to her elbow, then her shoulder, then the base of her neck.

She breathed his name, a sexy, throaty sound that made him want her to repeat it. He hurried now, longing for the taste and feel of her mouth on his. Her hands, free of his strong hold, traveled up into his hair, pulling his head toward her. He could feel her heart pounding. It only matched his own—uneven, thudding, sending shock waves through his system.

He nipped her bottom lip before sucking it in, then covered her mouth with his own.

Heaven. Pure, sweet heaven. He drank in her essence, filling himself with the taste, sight and sound of her, but it still wasn't enough. He wanted more. He wanted all of her.

He thrust his tongue into her mouth, plunging into her, driven by his need for her. Her own greedy tongue met him thrust for thrust.

Moaning, he pulled her closer, tangling his fingers in those incredible cinnamon curls.

His erection throbbed, demanding release. Not breaking the kiss, he pulled her onto his lap, taking care to swing her legs over his damaged knee. The weight of her against his straining arousal brought both satisfaction and an unmerciful desire to bury himself inside of her.

But not now. Not yet. Holding her like this felt too perfect. He couldn't mess it up by rushing her.

However, his pelvis tilted up on its own and pressed against her. Allison groaned, a deep, throaty sound of pleasure and longing. Tearing her mouth away, she sucked in deep breaths of air. Her hands traveled over his shoulders, then down his sides as she shifted her body to lie fully against him.

He could feel the moist heat of her apex even through the twisted sheet. He needed to thrust himself into her, to feel her slick heat wrap around him.

The temptation became too much, so he shifted her to his side and slid his fingers between her thighs. His groin protested the loss of her weight, but even in his foggy state, Jay knew he couldn't let things go too far too fast.

Her eagerness and unfettered responses to his touch warmed his heart. She seemed both childlike and all woman; he could swear that she showed astonishment at the waves of pleasure he saw on her face. How could she be that sexy and sensual, yet so innocent at the same time?

Even through her shorts, he sensed her aching, demanding need for him. Intrigued, he touched her and she pressed eagerly against his hand with a frenzied groan, rocking against his fingers.

Damn, he wanted to sink into her, feel her wetness. She was so responsive, so unabashedly sexy that he couldn't help but be mesmerized by her. His erection surged and throbbed; he threw his head back with a gasp, then ached to taste her. Gripping the waistband on her shorts, he unbuttoned them and jerked the zipper down. His hands followed the zipper's slide, searching for her wet, damp need.

"Jay!" She sucked in harshly as he made contact, pressing herself against his fingers, demanding that he enter her. Jay obliged, loving the way she drew him in deeply, then clenched around him. He could imagine doing the same with his penis; her hot tight pulsations would drive him beyond his wildest fantasies.

With his other hand, he tried remove her shorts, but she stopped him. He could feel her shyness and suddenly understood that she was uncomfortable with her body.

"You're so beautiful," he whispered, meaning every word. "I just want to see more."

She flushed, her smile holding embarrassment as he witnessed her struggle to accept his words at face value. "I'm just not comfortable. It's just that I—"

"Shhh," he said, kissing her lips in featherlight caresses that were meant to distract her but did massive damage to his self-control. "Give it time. You'll become more comfortable with me." Had he just implied they had a future? Yes, he had. He waited for that jolt of discomfort, of wanting to take flight. After all, he'd just met her. But instead, he knew he'd spoken the truth.

She smiled, but he could tell that she didn't quite buy it. He didn't blame her. He lifted a thumb to her cheek, tracing over her curved bone structure, delighting in the softness of her skin, in the flush of color that enhanced her beauty in a way no lotions or powders ever could.

"God, you're amazing," he whispered, tasting the base of her throat; her sweet flesh seemed to melt as his mouth sucked and nibbled. Her tiny moans of submission rocked him closer and closer to the edge. He felt in tune and passionately interwoven with her. Her every breath became his; her every shudder evoked a responding pulsation of his own.

He found her lips and tasted her as his fingers plunged into her. She thrust against his hand while her leg curled up over him, rubbing in rhythm against his distended arousal. It was too much; he couldn't hold himself back.

"Allison, if you don't..." His breath hissed out as her hand inched under her leg to press against him. "Allison, slow down. If you don't, I won't be able to stop what happens."

Her amazing blue eyes leapt up at him, their color intensified by passion. "But I don't want you to stop," she panted.

He kissed her, drawing her into him, then nipped at the tip of her tongue. She chuckled against his mouth, and then gasped as his hand renewed its stroking between her legs.

"Jay," He swallowed her voice with his mouth, and she clung to his lips, then pulled away. "There are too many clothes between us."

His unoccupied hand whisked over her breasts. With satisfaction, he watched her nipples harden. He smiled at her. "You're right, there's way too many—"

A loud knock reverberated through the room. "Yoo-hoo, Allison!" Birdie's voice rang out. Jay heard his front door sweep over the rug placed before it; she'd apparently let herself in.

The two almost-lovers jerked away from each other. Allison struggled to get off the bed, banging into Jay's knee in the process. With a strangled shout, he pitched away from her, but still caught her bottom with his shoulder and knocked her right off the bed onto the floor.

"I'm sorry!" she whispered, trying to stand and zip her shorts up at the same time. "Are you okay?"

Jay's breath hissed through his teeth as he fought to ride the pain through. "Oh, yeah, just peachy." Thankfully the pain had deflated his erection rapidly, or he would have been aching in too many places to deal with.

Allison jerked herself upright, snapped her shorts shut. Then she snatched up Jay's painkillers just as Birdie, complete with her Ping accessory cradled in her arms, walked into the room. Jay watched Allison's eyes skitter away from the landlady. He decided to gaze at his unexpected guest instead of lingering on Allison's guilt-ridden face and relishing how those crimson spots of mortified color had come to be there in the first place.

Birdie smiled brightly at Allison as she fumbled with the bottle's lid. "Hi, love. Are you all right? You seem a bit flushed." She turned her gaze onto Jay, and her smile vanished, transformed instead into a vague likeness of one of the faces on Mount Rushmore. He wasn't quite sure which one.

"I'm fine, Birdie." Allison brushed her disheveled hair from out of her face. "I thought you'd left for the night."

"I forgot my knitting needles on the chair, and I want to finish that sweater for Ping to wear to his next show." Picking the needles up off the chair, she juggled Ping onto one arm so she could hold them well away from the dog. For her efforts, Ping grunted, looking every inch the disgruntled monarch, although a very ugly one.

"Jay, you look pale." Yes, he could imagine that. His knee throbbed in excruciating rhythm.

"I banged my knee just a minute ago. Allison's getting me a painkiller." Good, Cantrall. Not a lie in there.

"Good idea," Birdie said. "You look like you need something. Well, I'm off." She cast one more worried glance toward Allison. "Are you sure you're all right? You do look hot."

Allison jerked her head in what Jay assumed was a nod, but looked more like a seizure to him. *Relax,* he willed her silently.

"Yes, I'm fine. It's a hot day, Birdie." Jay controlled a snort of disgust. Allison Leavitt wouldn't last long as a criminal. She sucked at lying.

She followed Birdie out of the bedroom, and when he heard the door closed, he figured she'd fled. He sank down into his pillow and let his eyes shut. He let his mind drift back to his near-lovemaking with Allison.

He couldn't remember the last time he'd felt so turned on and tuned in. What was it about her? Was it her smile, her quick wit, her beautiful eyes? Or could it be that touch-me/touch-me-not aura she wore like a cloak?

"Here." His eyes flew open to find Allison hovering over him, a glass of water in one hand, a painkiller in her other. She popped the pill in his mouth without warning, then held out the glass.

Jay propped himself up on an elbow, swallowing the pill with one large swig. He put the glass down on the nightstand, intending to pull Allison back into his arms and continue where he'd left off. But she stepped quickly out of reach.

"Allison?"

She didn't meet his eyes, but her voice gave a clear message. "No," She took another step back. "I can't."

"You mean you won't?" His anticipation dropped like a rock. Hadn't she felt the same things that he had?

The heat that flooded her face told him she'd been as moved as he over their kisses and caresses. Then why wouldn't she come back and enjoy more of the same?

"Give me one good reason."

Her hands slid through her hair, causing the already wild curls to tangle even more.

Damn. He wanted those to be his hands.

Her face scrunched up; he could see emotions battling inside her, but he didn't understand why.

Women made these things too complicated. To Jay, it was simple. If she wanted him, she should have him. Take him, do what she needed to do with him. But women didn't think about that. They pulled all these emotions and feelings and deeper meanings into everything. They took a good clean thing like sex and complicated it.

He didn't pay any attention to the niggling voice in his head that whispered that it might be more than sex to him, as well.

"I can't. I like the stuff we did, the…foreplay. But the rest, well, it's…it's disappointing. I don't need to do it to know it'll be disappointing."

Jay stared at her. He couldn't be more shocked. Disappointing? How could anyone think that sex was disappointing?

"Disappointing for whom?"

Her eyes widened, as if she felt affronted at his denseness. "For me. I've—" Her face deepened in color and she turned away from him.

"You've what?"

"I've never…" Her arms wrapped around her breasts and her back hunched. "I've never had an orgasm during sex."

"Then you've never been with a real man."

Without responding, she fled the room. Moments later he heard the apartment door slam shut.

Jay sighed and laid back into the pillow. He rubbed his hand over his mouth in frustration, but her female scent lingered on his hand. His groin tightened again in reaction. With a grunt of frustration, he pulled his hand away. Her words echoed in his mind.

I've never had an orgasm during sex.

How could he not take up a challenge like that?

Chapter Ten

Allison slammed the door to her apartment, then locked it and turned the deadbolt. Her chest heaved up and down in sharp pants. She didn't know if it was from sprinting from Jay's bedroom to her apartment or from her reaction to what had just happened with him.

Or if the ache she felt stemmed from disappointment.

She picked up the door chain to slide it in place, then stopped and stared at it. Stupid, stupid! Did she honestly think he'd charge after her and try to force his way in? Especially with his bum knee? Did she really need the locks to keep him at bay?

On the other hand, they'd slow her down if she got tempted to go back over there.

She slid the chain into place.

Sitting down on the futon, she cradled her face in her hands, her cool fingers a welcome contrast to her overheated skin. What on earth had just happened to her? She'd never behaved so wantonly and uncontrolled before.

She'd never been so turned on before.

Her body tingled at the thought of Jay's hands over her, touching her, exploring her body. Why did he affect her so? Was it because he embodied her image of Ben Stark so completely?

Or was it all Jay?

She ached deep inside. Her body demanded fulfillment, but part of her understood that with Jay, it would be more than sex. Something about him, despite his gruff exterior, spoke volumes to her. Maybe it was the vulnerability she'd glimpsed deep inside his eyes. Perhaps it was the tenderness with which he'd touched her. She didn't know.

If she were smart, she'd take care not to find out.

What was wrong with her? Was she really trying to live a fantasy, or was it something else, something more basic?

Could she be missing a man's touch? Maybe her feminine side needed more attention. After all, other than a few evenings a month pleasuring herself, she didn't give her womanly needs much thought. Perhaps she'd been reacting more out of an unbalanced hormonal problem than anything else.

Yes, that had to be it. It couldn't be anything else.

Satisfied with her conclusion, Allison decided to push the incident from her mind. She'd pretend as if nothing had happened, and Jay, being a bright man, would pick up on that and follow suit. In no time at all, they'd both forget.

Now, all she needed to do was convince her out-of-control libido.

🐾 🐾 🐾

An insistent ringing in his ear dragged Jay from a deep sleep. Morning sunlight slanted through the partially closed blinds. The jabbing ache in his knee reminded him of the previous day's occurrences. He'd forgotten the pain in his dreams. He'd gladly return there, if only to stop the ringing.

Identifying the sound as the phone, he fumbled for the receiver. He grunted an unwelcoming hello.

"Jay! Finally! I've been trying to get hold of you for over a week."

At his brother's voice, Jay leaned back into the pillow. "I left you messages. Didn't Mike tell you I called?" Mike was Jeff's agent. Jeff, an actor, currently made his living on a British soap opera; they'd been on location shooting an exotic Caribbean story line when Jay'd been shuffled off to Spokane and this Ping-infested apartment building.

"He left a message on my machine. I didn't think to call that until this morning, though, after I hunted down your partner and he filled me in on your transfer. Apparently I don't earn Mike enough money for him to bother calling me at the hotel. And my bloody mobile doesn't work in the Grand Caymans."

"'Bloody?' I think you've spent too much time in England, bro." Jay smiled; there were times he forgot about the benefits of being a twin, but those times were very rare. Even though a continent and an ocean separated them, Jay still considered Jeff his best friend.

Their parents, who now lived in San Diego, remarked from time to time that raising twins sometimes felt like watching an exclusive club, knowing they could never join. Jay and Jeff were close; sometimes he swore they were in each other's skin.

"Ahh, fink so, guv'nor? Me ol' mucker, me ol' mate?"

Jay chortled at Jeff's phony accent. The action cost him, however, as his knee twinged unforgivingly. He sucked in a breath, tamping down on the sharp throbbing.

"You okay, bro?" Jeff could always pick up on Jay's troubles; thousands of miles didn't change his intuitive knowledge.

"I banged up my knee a bit; should be fine in a few days. How's the gig going over there?"

Jeff's grin could be heard through the phone lines. "Great. I was just voted the sexiest soap star. Not bad for a Yank, eh?"

"Does this mean I could get lucky if I come over to London and pretend to be you?" It was a longstanding rivalry between the two: women seemed to prefer Jeff over Jay, and usually that didn't bother him. Except for the last time. She'd used him to get an introduction to his brother; her deception not only threatened the department's reputation but his career.

Jeff laughed, the sound a mirror of Jay's own. "I'd love to have you here. If you're off for a few, why don't you come over?"

Thoughts of London enticed him. It would be good to see Jeff, and there were no nasty little dogs waiting to trip him up over there. But the words of acceptance wouldn't come; Jay couldn't put a finger on why he felt reluctant.

It couldn't have anything to do with Allison Leavitt, could it? Or those incredible few minutes they'd shared?

He didn't know if he wanted to know the answer. Several moments passed while Jay struggled with a reply to his brother's question.

He remembered kissing and holding Allison. Just the memories caused him to harden. She'd shimmered with life and he'd soaked that in. He'd spent the night dreaming about her; hot steamy dreams that he'd wake up from, panting and hard with need for her. Then he'd fall asleep again, only to find himself caught up in yet another passion-filled dream. Until the phone had brought him bouncing back to reality.

"Jay? What the hell's going on over there?"

Jay barked a laugh. "I don't know what you mean." But he had a good hunch.

"You sound uneasy. I can hear pain, but there's something else. Something that has you off kilter. Is it this transfer?"

A knock sounded. Calling out 'Come in!' to who he hoped would be Allison, Jay tried to answer his brother's question. "I'm not taking being injured very well, that's all. And yes, I don't like being transferred. L.A.'s my home. I need to get back there."

"Jay?" Allison's voice floated through the living room. Her soft feminine tones didn't go unnoticed by Jeff's sharp ears.

Jeff rarely missed anything where Jay was concerned. Unfortunately, distance didn't lesson his intuition. "Ah, now the picture becomes clear. You have female trouble."

"No," The denial burst out sharper than he'd meant. "That's a neighbor who's helping me out until I get back on my feet. Nothing more." Yet. After last night, though…

"Yet?" Uncannily, Jeff echoed his own errant thought. "Okay, bro, I'll let you go. But think about my offer. You can always bring her with you."

"Not very likely."

He felt Jeff's mental shrug. "Then come alone. I'll hook you up with a couple of lovelies who'll knot your knickers in a bunch in no time, mate." Jay laughed as he caught movement. Allison. He looked up, to be pierced by those deep blue eyes.

He barely acknowledged his brother's goodbye as he hung up the phone, still smiling at the conversation. Allison looked like sunshine today, in a bright yellow tank top paired with loose jean shorts. Her unruly curls were tied up haphazardly on top of her head. An errant strand of hair brushed the curve of her cheek, accentuating her womanly appeal.

"Good morning." She leaned against the doorway, trying to hide the nervousness he saw lurking in her eyes.

"Morning." Jay shifted in the bed, wincing when the movement jarred his sore knee. Damn. He needed a painkiller. Right after a trip to the bathroom.

Allison witnessed his wince, "I really am sorry about your getting hurt. I wish I could make it up to you."

Her words brought back images that Jay couldn't dwell on or Allison would quickly know how she affected him, considering only a sheet covered him. "I'll tell you what. If you quit apologizing, I'll let you try to make amends."

"Oh? And how do you propose I do that?" she asked. He didn't miss the tone of suspicion that coated her words.

"Breakfast would be nice."

"Oh, gosh!" Her hand clapped to her mouth. "I have breakfast for you, and I forgot it in the apartment! Birdie made Belgian waffles this morning and I have quite a few left. They've probably gone cold by now. I'll have to zap them in the microwave." Her face brightened. "How about I walk you out to the pool? You can enjoy the morning sunshine, and I'll bring your breakfast out to you. It should be fairly quiet and Birdie's garden really is lovely at this time of day."

Her enthusiasm to please him warmed him. *Why not?* he reasoned. He had nothing else to do.

"All right," he agreed. "But I'll walk myself out. I need to make a pit stop first."

She blushed slightly at his statement. Jay grinned. Who would have thought a woman who'd been so passionately responsive would be embarrassed at the mention of bodily functions?

He decided not to mention last night. If he did, she'd probably scald her skin into a permanent red.

Her voice warbled slightly as she spoke. "I'll meet you out there in a few minutes." She wiggled her fingers at him and left in a rush.

After a visit to the bathroom and a thorough face washing and teeth brushing, along with a change into some loose gray shorts, an LAPD tank top and the brace he was beginning to hate, he headed out to the pool, carrying the latest Robert Tyler book in his hand. He liked mystery novels, and this writer never disappointed.

He stopped along the way to adjust one of the brace's long Velcro straps. He'd have to cut those later, he thought, or they'd start catching on things.

Straps flapping in the wind, he hobbled slowly along the pool. This was a good idea, he thought as the sun warmed his skin. A tasty breakfast, a relaxing read by the pool, and the peaceful sounds of a summer garden. And no yipping—

Yap! Yap Yap!

Jay groaned. It couldn't be...

It was.

Before he could react, Ping, clad in a bright yellow T-shirt with an orange happy face on the back, reached him, barking furiously, his bell jingling all the while. Jay spun around, trying to keep his attacker in front of him, but the little dog whirled about him, front legs lifting off the ground with each aggravated yip.

Spinning became a mistake. The dangling strap of Velcro enticed Ping, and he leapt for it, snatching the material in his strong little teeth as his ten-pound body slammed into Jay's knee. Jerking away from the impact, Jay lost his balance.

With a sinking feeling, he felt himself fall backwards. Windmilling his arms, trying to stave off the inevitable, he hit the water hard. A sense of doom engulfed him the same time the water did.

Jay could feel a weight still anchored to the brace; peering through the water, he saw Ping holding tenaciously to the strap, six feet under water.

Even drowning, the dog would have his revenge.

Chapter Eleven

"Jay!" Dropping the plate she carried, Allison rushed to the pool. Could he swim with that brace on?

"Ping!" Birdie shrieked, coming out her French doors. "Where's Ping?"

Water churned as Allison reached the pool. Kicking off her sandals, she prepared to dive in just as an arm broke the surface a yard away. Like a scene from King Arthur, the hand pointed straight up, displaying its prize: a growling, choking Ping, who twisted in fury.

Jay's head popped up as he gasped, his free arm flailing for the pool edge. Allison grasped his hand, pulling him closer.

Ping landed with a plop on the pool's rim, where he sat, a sad mass of wet T-shirt and drooping crest, hacking feebly.

Birdie reached her pet, her muumuu-clad bosom heaving from running. "He's choking," she shrieked. "He can't breathe!"

Jay pulled himself up onto the concrete next to the dog. Without a word he reached for Ping, who in his distress, didn't put up a fight. Jay pulled the wet shirt off the dog, then began to vigorously run both hands up and down his rib cage.

The dog coughed once, twice; the hacking stopped. Then he snapped at Jay's hand.

Jerking away from Ping, Jay curled a lip. "He's fine," he declared, then rolled onto his back. Allison could tell that although Ping might be fine, the fall had strained Jay's small strength reserve.

"Ping!" Birdie snatched up the dog and began to dry him with the edge of her flowing red muumuu. "Jay, I'm sorry. Usually he's so friendly and patient, but he doesn't seem to like you. Thank you for saving him," she blubbered, holding the trembling animal to her chest. "Come on, let's go get you dried off."

Allison crouched by Jay, who'd stretched out alongside the pool, injured knee bent slightly in the brace. "Are you all right?" she breathed.

Eyes closed, Jay didn't move. "You dropped my breakfast, didn't you?"

"Umm…" Allison looked over at the plate, shattered against the ground, the waffles scattered. "Yes, I guess I did." When she'd seen Jay fall into the pool, breaking one of her plates had been the least of her worries. All she'd thought of was if he could swim with the brace on. If he'd drowned…

She ignored the ache that spread into her heart at the thought.

"I was looking forward to some waffles. And my book?"

Allison's gaze searched the poolside; with an air of finality she glanced into the pool.

"On the bottom."

"Too bad. I was almost finished. Now I'll never know if Jared Vale will reach the bomb in time to save Stephanie."

Allison eyed him; his tank top molding to his broad chest, emphasizing his well-sculpted muscles. Her throat dried out; she couldn't swallow. Her breath was shallow in her lungs.

She must be catching the flu.

"My knee hurts, but not as bad as I thought it would," Jay said. "My finger hurts; damned dog actually bit me under water."

Kneeling over him, she studied the planes of his face. She didn't see any signs of pain, and his bizarre sense of humor after his dunking confused her.

Jay glanced up at her. "Allison…"

"Yes?"

"You smell good. Like syrup and shampoo."

She couldn't handle this flirtatious side of Jay. "Did you hit your head? You're acting strange." Where was the frown he always wore? Why wasn't he snarling like he usually did?

Jay smiled, a small twist of his lips that fluttered her pulse. "I'm fine, but I learned something while struggling underwater with my pint-sized attacker."

"And what's that?"

"That I don't want to meet my Maker without having done this again." Reaching cool, wet fingers behind her neck, he pulled her down to meet his lips.

His kiss was soft, tender, almost curious. It wasn't the kind of kiss that should have coiled her into knots and made her long for more. But it did. At the impact of his mouth, she found herself falling into him, losing herself in the contact.

She deepened the kiss, taking in the taste of him. She tried to define what these sensations were that coursed through her. Heat. Sizzle. Need. The scent of man and aftershave drove away all coherent thoughts, except those of Jay, and how well they fit together, how good it felt to be crushed up against his wet form, how—

"Allison."

He pushed up on her shoulders; his voice penetrated through her fogged brain. She couldn't understand why he'd stopped kissing her; she leaned into him again.

"You need to get off me. I can't breathe."

"Oh," She rolled off him swiftly. "I'm sorry. Did I hurt you?" How unromantic! She'd been sent into outer orbit while her passion killed the object of her desire!

"No, but I'm feeling a bit…lightheaded," Jay struggled to prop himself up on his elbows. Grinning wickedly, he continued, "We could move to somewhere more comfortable—like my apartment."

Shocked at his leering smile, outrage bubbled inside her. Here, she'd felt the earth move, and Jay thought this was a mere interlude to sex?

What did she expect? After all, he was a man, and hadn't she learned the hard way all men were pigs?

She didn't dwell on the idea that she'd not helped her case by responding so wildly to his caresses last night. No, he shouldn't just presume she wanted to hop into bed with him!

Shoving away from him, her eyes flashed daggers at him. "I'll go get you breakfast. And a towel. You could use some drying up."

"Allison—"

She ignored him, traveling swiftly away from him. How could she be so stupid?

🐈 🐈 🐈

How could he be so stupid? A beautiful woman was kissing him, and he thought he needed to breathe? Then he'd actually leered at her? No wonder she'd fled!

"I blew that," he muttered to himself. Struggling up, he regained his feet, then hobbled over to a chaise lounge. Carefully lowering himself down and stretching his injured leg out as much as the soggy brace allowed, he castigated himself for his treatment of her.

But he hadn't wanted it to end. He wanted to explore her softness, her desires; he wanted to learn if she moaned when he kissed the base of her neck or if she preferred sensual nibbling on the ear. Now he'd blown it with his eagerness. And his lack of sensitivity.

Closing his eyes, he leaned back into the chair, grappling over how to fix things. Did he try to apologize, or pretend it never happened? If he asked for forgiveness, she might think that he regretted kissing her and that was far from the true. He wanted to do it again. Badly. The strength of his need caused him to wonder if she'd like L.A. on a long-term basis.

And if he said nothing? Then her anger could fester and she'd feel bitterness toward him.

Either way, he lost.

He recalled her shocking statement from last night. *I've never had an orgasm during sex.* He could only imagine that her former lovers never took the time to learn about what turned her on, and never bothered to teach her how to get the most out of making love. He knew he could initiate her into the best of the craft. Last night, he would have bet she'd been only moments away from a bone-shattering orgasm. Yes, he'd take his time with her, concentrate on giving her pleasure, and show her that sex never needed to be disappointing.

Light scratching on his uninjured leg jerked his eyes open. Glancing down, he saw Ping quietly staring up at him. A cutesy blue Hawaiian shirt that sported little female dogs wearing hula skirts had replaced his wet T-shirt; his collar featured a large shiny medallion studded with rhinestones. Birdie stood several yards away, watching carefully. Her features were carved in stone; Jay couldn't discern her thoughts. That bothered him; her usual openness was absent.

Jay eyed Ping with trepidation. True, he wasn't barking at him; rather, he cocked his head, studying Jay. But this one minor improvement didn't lead him to believe that Ping didn't mean to cause him harm.

With a small whine, Ping leapt onto Jay's lap. Stunned, Jay's hands flew up in the air.

"Hey, guy, a little too close! I don't think I like you this near to my...tender spots. Jump on down, there's a good boy!" The Chinese Crested's plans became clear: swatting a paw through the air, Ping whined. He held his paw out to Jay; when Jay didn't respond, he scratched Jay's chest, then swatted the air again.

"He's trained to shake hands," Birdie said.

Comprehending, Jay held his hand out. Ping solemnly placed his tiny paw on his palm. Jay squeezed it lightly, then let go. With a satisfied sigh, Ping lay down on Jay's lap, still studying him as if gauging the man's demeanor.

Ping scratched at the collar of his shirt. A few grunts accompanied the back paw's movements as the dog attempted to dislodge the shirt.

"That thing bothers you, huh? Man, I don't blame you. Some of the stuff that you wear isn't fit for any guy, even a hairless one," Jay lowered his voice so Birdie couldn't overhear him. He'd learned his lesson there. Irritating the landlady didn't bode well for his living arrangement. "If I had to wear a rhinestone collar, I think my manhood would shrivel up and die. And this shirt isn't much better. I mean, little dogs in hula skirts? Is that supposed to do something for you? Is that her idea of a drinking shirt? You're not a bad-looking dog. For a rat-dog, that is. And it is summer. Why can't she let you go shirtless?"

Ping's head cocked and his triangular ears perked up, as if agreeing to every word Jay spoke.

"I'd take that shirt off you, pal, but I really don't want to get bitten again."

At the word 'off' Ping whined and scooted forward, his tiny paws flexing out toward Jay.

"You want me to take it off? Am I understanding you right?"

Again Ping whined. Yup, he understood him clearly. The question remained: did he trust the dog enough to attempt what Ping wanted?

The answer: definitely not. However, he'd have to try. Where were leather gloves when he needed them?

During his uniformed years, Jay'd worked closely with K9 units and had learned how to move and behave around them. The only difference was that those dogs were highly trained police officers. This dog didn't have the discipline. And his teeth, although much smaller, were sharper. *That* Jay knew from personal experience.

Moving slowly and talking in soothing tones, Jay grasped the hem of the shirt and carefully pulled it upwards. Ping helped by sitting up and lifting his front legs one at a time, letting the shirt come off without incident. Jay heaved a sigh of relief—until Ping's head moved toward his hand in a lightning-fast move.

And deposited a lick.

Smiling, Jay stroked Ping's back tentatively. The dog grinned at him, if indeed dogs could smile.

Jay didn't dare look in Birdie's direction. He could only imagine her reaction to his undressing her pet.

Out of the corner of his eye, Jay saw Allison stepping through her French doors, carrying a plate, a glass of orange juice, a towel, and an ice bag. Under one arm, she clutched a fat book that resembled the one that now resided at the bottom of the pool.

"Food's coming, pal. And hopefully I can apologize without making things worse. Do you have any advice?"

Ping cocked his head. An ambiguous reply at best. Obviously he was on his own.

"I see you two've made up." Allison smiled at him, but it seemed forced.

Jay grimaced. "I don't think I had a choice. It was either that or face the wrath of Ping."

Laughter gurgled in Allison's throat. "Yes, considering where's he's sitting, that could be rather painful."

"Yes, that same thought crossed my mind," Jay responded, his tones dry. He observed her as she set the items she'd brought on a nearby glass-topped end table and dragged it closer. Despite her laughter a moment ago, he noticed that she held herself stiffly, her movements awkward and stilted. He didn't need to be a master at reading body language to know an angry woman when he saw one.

Did he dare try to explain his earlier behavior? If he didn't, would her anger grow and build up inside her until it bubbled over? Or would it dissipate and fade away? He didn't know Allison well, but he would hazard a bet that fading anger wasn't one of her virtues. All right then, an apology and an explanation would be best.

Glancing around, he watched Birdie go back into her apartment. Either he'd upset her by removing Ping's Hawaiian shirt or she felt Ping could be entrusted in Jay's care. In either case, he and Allison were now alone.

"I wanted—"

Uh, oh. He'd spoken too soon. Paige came out of the building, aimed in their direction like a heat-seeking missile. Dressed in a tight skirt and form-fitting blouse, with tall stiletto heels, Jay could tell she was on a mission. If he didn't miss his guess, he'd say that said-mission involved a man.

Jay could have groaned his frustration. Why did she have to show up now? He needed to get rid of her—and fast—before he lost the chance to apologize.

Ping's ears pricked up as Paige approached. Jay could feel a growl erupting from deep inside the dog.

"Ping," The dog flicked at ear at him, but continued his growl. Apparently Ping disliked Paige more than he disliked Jay. "Take a rest, pal, or the shirt goes back on."

The growl died, replaced by a whimper, then a shuffling of Ping's body until his head plopped down on his paws as he watched the dark-haired woman arrive.

Paige eyed Ping with clear dislike. "I thought the little road-kill hated you."

Jay shrugged. "Apparently sharing a near-death experience with someone can change even a dog."

Paige's eyebrows flew into her bangs. "What are you talking about?" Impatiently she waved her hand. "Never mind. If that dog's involved, I don't want to know. Al, can I talk to you?"

If Allison escaped with Paige, Jay'd never get his apology out. At least, not in a timely manner; Jay knew timing could be everything.

"Call him."

Paige turned startled eyes toward him. "Excuse me?"

"Pearce. Call him." Couldn't the woman follow instructions?

Paige whirled toward Allison. "Have you been talking to him about me?"

Allison's eyes widened. "Paige, I never said –"

"Allison didn't say anything to me. Just do us all a favor and give him a call. Please. Before anyone else gets hurt." He stared pointedly at his knee, hoping she'd get the hint. Apparently the point wasn't taken; she stared back in confusion. Jay sighed; why couldn't talking to women ever be easy? "He wouldn't have asked you to meet him if he didn't want to talk to you."

"I don't need him telling me anything." Paige glared at him. "I figured out why he wanted to see me. To tell me he's getting married."

Jay's laugh rumbled. "Hardly." He slanted her a grin. "He could do that over the phone. What he wants to tell you needs to be done in person."

"Oh." Both women stared at him, then at each other.

"Paige, I think you need to go." Allison punctuated the last word with an emphatic shooing motion.

Paige nodded wildly. Color bloomed on her cheeks as she backed away rapidly. "Yes, I think you're right." She turned to leave, then stopped abruptly. Clicking over to Jay, she leaned down and kissed him on the cheek.

"Thanks. You're a doll. I'll tell Pearce what a great partner he has."

Jay nearly choked. Pearce wouldn't thank him for his interference. "No, don't. Let him believe you came to your senses on your own."

Paige giggled. "You're right, I'll do that. Thanks again."

Wiggling her fingers in Allison's direction, she made a hasty retreat.

Jay watched her for a moment, amazed that she didn't fall over on those thin heels. Turning his attention to Allison, he found her smiling down at him.

"That was a nice thing you just did. She's been stressing over it…"

He waved her words away. He needed to get this done; he hated leaving things half-finished. "I did it to get rid of her so I could talk to you. Could you sit down, please?"

Allison remained standing, her arms crossed over her chest. Not a good sign. "So you weren't being nice and thoughtful?"

"If it makes you think better of me, then yes, I was being very kind and thoughtful." At her frown, he realized his teasing banter wasn't winning any points. "Allison, I only wanted to talk to you alone. I think we need to clear the air between us."

"Oh?" One brow arched up as her crossed arms tightened. Really bad sign. This kept going from dismal to worse. "And what exactly do we need to clear?"

"I wanted to apologize." At her unbending stare, he added, "For what happened."

"You mean, you're sorry you kissed me?"

Okay, worse just got even deeper. "No, I don't mean that. I enjoyed the kiss. I loved the kiss. I wanted to continue—"

"Oh, you made it clear that you wanted to continue. In your bedroom!" Her eyes blazed brighter than the sky; if he hadn't been the recipient of her outrage, he would have been dazzled by her beauty. As it was, he sincerely doubted his ability to diffuse her anger.

What was it his dad used to say? A man could never understand a woman. He could only hope to survive one.

Here was his chance to live up to his father's hopes.

"No. I wanted us have more privacy—"

"So you could what? See how fast you could coerce me into bed?"

Okay, he was teetering on the edge of hell, waiting for her to shove him. Time to go on the defensive. "I don't remember being the only one in that kiss."

She flushed. "I admit, I got carried away. But I didn't offer to move it indoors. You did. You were reading way too much into it to assume I wanted it to go anywhere with you."

"You're reading too much into my offer if you think that I wanted to complicate my life by sleeping with you," he responded.

"Oh?" she huffed. "Now I'm not worth sleeping with?"

Her reply stunned him, jerking him upright and startling Ping right off his lap. The little dog barked once in protest, then trotted off in search of Birdie.

"I didn't say that! I said—"

"I know full well what you said. That I'm not worth complicating your life over!" She glared down at him. "Well, remember this, pal! It'll be a cold day in hell before I let you come close enough to get another chance at any sort of complication!"

Her anger hardened his resolve; he didn't need to deal with this. Forget the apology; Allison Leavitt was too much trouble, despite the fact she sent his libido over the edge more easily than any other woman he'd ever met.

"You're being hysterical," he informed her coolly, "And I'm not going to sit here and argue with you. You're right about one thing, though," he added as he closed his eyes and leaned back in the lounge chair. "It'll be a cold day before—"

A rattle cut off his words as something incredibly chilly and wet poured into his lap.

"What the—!" Jay roared as the upended bag of ice found its target—his crotch. The cold shocked him out of the lounge chair and he awkwardly fell on the concrete. Outraged, he turned to lambaste the woman who'd just assaulted him.

But nothing was left of her except her French door slamming shut. Nothing left for him to deal with but his frozen male ego.

Chapter Twelve

Words flew into the computer as Allison typed madly and fumed. How dare he? Who did he think he was? Why, Ben Stark would never behave that way toward a woman!

Her fingers stilled as she realized what she'd just thought. Was she really confusing Jay with Ben? Were they really that much alike?

Ben Stark, her macho hero, practiced a 'love-them-and-leave-them' attitude toward women. He never stuck around for more than a few nights, and showed loyalty to only Emily, his long-suffering partner who secretly loved him, but never told him. But Ben's heart did belong to one woman, whom he'd met years before in Allison's first book, and although she'd disappeared, to only be glimpsed in the subsequent books, Ben had never forgotten her.

She couldn't see Jay pining for any woman. No, he'd never return for a woman, nor would he hunt for her. He'd move on, dismissing her from his thoughts just as he'd dismissed Taffy.

Ben rarely showed emotion to anyone but Emily. He kept everything bottled inside; his adversaries never knew his thoughts unless he told them. Jay, however, had expressive eyes, although his face gave little away. She found herself reading his eyes like a book. Anger, humor, passion, she recognized them all.

No, Jay definitely had some assets that Ben Stark didn't. The few glimpses she'd seen of his sense of humor had sent her heart fluttering.

That little-boy grin he flashed on rare occasions…well, that should be listed as a lethal weapon. And his kiss…

He'd surprised her with his kiss that morning, but her reaction had startled her more. One touch and all her bones had turned to jelly; all the reasons why she didn't need a man had melted away until there'd been just her and him and the way their flesh had melded together, the way his tongue had plunged into the depths of her mouth. She'd tried to convince herself that last night had been a fluke. Now she knew better.

A shaky breath escaped her lips, and she stared at the blinking black cursor on the screen. If she kept this up, she'd be a gibbering mess of nerves in a matter of days. Kiss him; don't kiss him. Like him; hate him. She needed to make up her mind.

Or just stay away. After all, he came from L.A. and she hated L.A. After living there for half her life, she'd seen the worst of the city—the smog, dirt, traffic, angry people, road rage, selfishness. She had no desire to ever move back there.

How could she even consider getting involved with a man like Jay Cantrall? There was no future for them. She couldn't imagine moving away from here, and a hard-nosed cop like him belonged in a big city, not in Spokane, which still felt like a smaller town.

And where did thoughts of a future come from? She loved her freedom and not having to worry about another human being. So why did she agonize about whether or not he'd stay in Spokane? If she thought practically about it, his leaving would be a good ending to a short-term affair. Her response to him told her one thing clearly: it had been way too long since she'd made love. She needed to correct that, and soon. Apparently battery-operated substitutes didn't quite cut it for her feminine needs.

So why not take Jay up on his offer? Could she ask for a better situation, if she seriously wanted a fling? After all, she'd have to look long and hard to find a more attractive prospect. What better way to get her over-active libido under control than a few weeks of wild sex? Then she'd be immune for a few more years from the craving she felt for Jay. No, strike that. Not just Jay. Any man. This was merely the reaction of her sex-starved body to a rather tempting stimulus.

She sucked in a deep breath and let it out slowly. Okay, fine. She'd do it. She'd have a hot, steamy affair and enjoy it while it lasted.

As long as she kept her heart out of the deal, a short fling would be ideal. But that could be the kicker. How did she keep from falling in love with a man who could kiss like that?

🐈 🐈 🐈

"Hey, buddy," the voice over the phone said when Jay responded with the obligatory 'hello.' He recognized his former partner, Stan Brown's, voice. "Are you missing L.A. yet?"

Funny; if Stan had asked that same question three days ago, Jay would have given him an emphatic 'yes.' He loved the contrasts found in L.A.; the glamour, the grittiness. But now all he could think of was how he'd always wonder what might happen with Allison if he stuck around Spokane.

Considering that she wasn't speaking to him, it probably wouldn't be much.

"Hello? Jay, are you listening?"

Shaking his head free of thoughts of that tempting bundle of contradictions living next door, Jay apologized. "Sorry. What were you saying?" He sat up in bed, focusing all his thoughts on Stan's words.

"I thought you'd be more excited. You're off the hook. Melanie Rogers finally admitted that you never knew she was married or to whom. This happened after she accused you of asking her to have her husband put in a good word with the captain for your promotion. That got into the papers, by the way."

"What?" Stan had his full attention now. He'd never asked Melanie to do anything for him during their short two-week fling. Hell, he'd never known she'd been acquainted with the assistant district attorney, let alone married to him.

"Relax, she recanted almost immediately when it became obvious that implicating you wasn't wise. I told her quite clearly that not only would I prove she lied but I'd make sure she suffered the consequences for slander."

Jay's chest constricted at his partner's loyalty. "Thanks, pal. I owe you."

"Yes, you do. And you'll owe me even more for this: the Captain's agreed that you could come home whenever you're ready. He's pretty sure he can reverse the transfer with a phone call."

Home. His exile could be over today. But instead of the relief he should have experienced, Jay found himself making up reasons to stay.

Pearce needed a partner. His knee needed time to heal. He'd signed a month's lease on this place. Allison needed...

What did Allison need? Love, passion, romance? Him. She needed him. She needed him to teach her the better side of sex.

All he had to do was convince her.

"There's a small hitch, Stan. I injured my knee chasing a suspect yesterday, so I'm out of commission for a while."

"Damn, that's rough. How long are you sidelined?"

"At least a week." A week should give him enough time to figure out where he stood with Allison.

"Not a problem. You can come home and straddle a desk until your knee's up to real work." Stan laughed softly at his own joke.

"This is great news. Thanks for letting me know, and I appreciate your helping me out like you did."

"But…" Stan trailed the word off, waiting for Jay's refusal.

Jay smiled; Stan knew him too well. Partners for the last four years, they'd gotten to the point of finishing their sentences. "But I have unfinished business here that I need to take care of."

"I get you, man. I'll let the captain know you're recuperating and you'll give him a call later."

Anyone else would have been digging his nose into Jay's business. But Stan didn't ask, and for that, Jay felt grateful. His attraction for Allison was still too new to share with others.

After hanging up the phone, he stretched out on the bed, trying to decide on his next move. Did he call her, hobble over there, or just bide his time for a day or two? Yeah, give her some time to cool down, then perhaps send her some flowers. A few days to let her calm down would be a good idea. Heck, he'd tried the apology thing, and all that had gotten him was a frozen appendage.

In the meantime, he'd have to figure out how to get around. The doctor had stated in no uncertain terms he couldn't drive. Spokane didn't have taxis hanging around like downtown L.A. He'd have to—

"Jay?"

His heart slammed against his ribcage. Allison was here, in his apartment. By his estimate, he had about three seconds to decide what to say!

🐈 🐈 🐈

"Jay?" Allison walked into the apartment tentatively, her heart in her throat. She didn't know what to say to him; how do you announce to a man that you've decided to take up his offer of a fling?

Her hands shook as she entered the bedroom; gripping the book she carried more tightly, she smiled widely at him as he slowly sat up.

She forced her voice to sound normal as she wondered: *how do you go about seducing a man?*

"How…" Darn it, did her voice squeak? She tried again. "How are you feeling?" Placing the book on his nightstand, she willed a casual smile to her lips.

"Fine," he sat up straighter on the bed, patting the space next to him, "Please sit. My neck's a bit stiff and it hurts to look up at you."

"Oh." She planted herself next to him. Okay, she'd been looking for a reason to get close to him, and he'd handed it to her. Now what? How did one start a seduction?

She looked down at her clothes. Her choice of attire didn't help set the mood. How could anyone consider a yellow tank top and baggy shorts sexy? She should've thought ahead. Okay, her thinking ahead would have meant going all the way to the mall; nothing in her wardrobe screamed hot and tasty.

Her nerve was rapidly vanishing and she reminded herself sternly that he'd kissed her earlier while she'd been wearing similar clothes. If she was so repulsive, he wouldn't have done that, would he?

Of course, he'd just nearly drowned. His last kiss could be attributed to his near-death experience.

At that ego-deflating thought, Allison seriously considered dashing for the door. As her impulse became a definite plan, Jay laughed softly, a deep, rich laugh that hung in the air and froze her to the bed.

The sound felt like silk sliding over her skin. It curled her stomach and initiated funny tremors deep down…there. Her breath hissed out through her teeth. As the sensation tingled all the way to her toes, she turned toward him.

"What's so funny?"

His silver eyes danced. "Here I am, with one of the most beautiful women I've ever seen sitting on the bed with me, and I'm too damn sore to take advantage of it."

"Oh." He thought she was beautiful? Her face glowed with pleasure. From someone else, she'd have wondered if the compliment was sincere, but from Jay, that thought didn't occur to her at all. He didn't strike her as the type to toss words around, unless they were scathing.

While concocting her wild plan of seduction, she'd forgotten about his injury and his latest adventure. Of course he wasn't up to doing anything today; he'd almost drowned, for heaven's sake!

She smiled brightly, determined to make the best of things. She'd rethink this rash idea, hopefully come to her senses and he'd never be the wiser.

"I'm sorry about earlier," he told her. "I did enjoy kissing you. I suggested moving into here because I simply wanted to hold you while I kissed you. And I didn't want to embarrass you in front of your neighbors. But even that was presuming too much, and I apologize."

"And I'm sorry. I was being too sensitive." She shared a smile with him; it felt good, it felt right. She liked what his brighter mood did to his features. In fact, his entire demeanor seemed lighter, friendlier. She liked that a lot.

"I wanted to ask you something," he said, a tempting dimple at the corner of his mouth catching her eye. A tremor flashed through her apex, and she nearly gasped in pleasure. Oh, my, she did enjoy this version of Jay much more. Even better than anything she'd imagined with Ben Stark.

"Oh?" She fantasized tasting that dimple, running her mouth over that finely sculpted cheekbone…

Jay chuckled. "Allison, you're doing that fish thing again."

Her mouth closed. Firmly.

Jay laughed. "I need a serious distraction. Something mind-blowing would be nice."

"Excuse me?" Her mouth opened and closed again; she clamped it shut. Did he read her mind and know she had sex on the brain?

His smile widened at her reaction. "No, I don't mean that."

Darn, she thought.

"I'm going a bit stir-crazy being cooped up. I'm normally an active guy. I usually run and work out, but I'm being told to take it easy the first week or so. It's not sitting well with me, lying around all day. Any suggestions?"

"I…" Oh, yes, she had suggestions! But she couldn't bring herself to voice them. She felt her face infuse with heat, and she knew Jay's eagle eyes wouldn't miss that. But luckily he misunderstood.

"You're busy. A date?"

"No." No, no date. She'd be hard pressed to remember his name, the last man she'd dated after she and Nick had broken up. But she was supposed to be working, instead of sitting here trying to talk herself into making moves on this man.

"I do have something I need to do today, but it can wait."

"Tell me about it. Maybe I can tag along."

Only Birdie knew about her involvement with the soon-to-open spinal trauma center. To open it to public knowledge would be to expose her past mistakes and lifestyle to scrutiny—another reason she didn't seek publicity as her writing alter ego, Al Leavitt. Better that the world consider the author a strange recluse than discover that he was really a woman who'd hurt a young boy and never quite made up for it.

"I help out from time to time at this place. Kind of a volunteer thing." There. She'd covered up her involvement and made it sound boring at the same time.

But apparently Jay found boring things exciting. His eyes sparkled with interest.

"Tell me more. What kind of volunteering do you do?"

Was he for real? Or was he trying to impress her with his attention? No, Jay wouldn't worry about impressing anyone. He might want to get to know someone better, but she sincerely doubted he worried too much about what others thought of him.

"It's a pediatric spinal cord injury center. It's not open yet, but it will be soon. I..." What should she say? *I wrote large checks from my royalties and helped get funding from state and private agencies. I chose doctors and nurses who had the best expertise to give these people a fighting chance to get back on their feet.*

No, she couldn't say that. "I've been helping them get organized. It takes a lot of effort to get a place like that up and running."

"I can imagine." He actually looked impressed. "So what will they do there? Physical therapy?"

"It'll be more extensive than that. They'll work with the patient as soon as possible after the injury occurs. Hopefully within hours. They'll provide surgery, recommendations, rehab and long-term follow-up. We'll also provide resources for doctors to help them provide the best possible treatment for their patients. We'll be linked with a national network of clinics similar to this one, and—"

"You said 'we.'" Jay cocked his head slightly. She felt those unwavering eyes probing into her.

"I did?"

"You did."

"Oh. Well, I guess I'm feeling a bit of ownership. Is that wrong?" Ownership, heck. It went deeper than that. She'd worked hard to get this clinic to Spokane, all the while making sure to stay out of the spotlight. Soon it would be open, and she'd be able to convince herself she'd made up for the damage she'd done that boy all those years ago.

"Your face lights up when you talk about it. You really dig this place."

Heat tingeing her cheeks, she nodded. She felt uncomfortable being so easily read. Yet somehow it felt good. His bothering to understand her made it feel like somehow he was interested, that maybe he cared. She liked that feeling. She liked it maybe a little too much.

"I do enjoy it," she admitted. "It's knowing that this place can make a huge difference when it truly matters. When someone's at their lowest point, the clinic can give them hope and give them their future back." Like someone had to her, when she'd landed on her back and found herself crippled and all alone. Someone like Birdie.

Again, Jay read her too well. "You sound like you're speaking from experience."

Panic hit her. She didn't want to go there right now and talk about those horrifying months, and all the pain she'd gone through. Thoughts of seduction fled as she searched frantically in her mind for a way to escape.

Jay, however, had other plans.

"Let's go." Jay pushed himself off the bed awkwardly, leaving Allison feeling bereft. He levered himself upright, then held his hand out to her. Without even thinking twice, she placed her fingers on his palm. Awareness sizzled through her; the mere heat from his fingers caused tremors deep inside her. *Whoa, baby.* She had it bad. Her panic fled, unable to linger as need filled her.

"Go? Go where?"

"To your volunteer place. I want to see it."

"But...but..." Her mind whirled. He wanted to see the center. Now?

Pulled up onto her feet, she found herself standing very close to him. Too close. She could smell his light, spicy aftershave and see the faint dark blond stubble on his face. She could imagine how it would feel against her. Rough. Erotic. *Oh, my.*

She trembled; their earlier kiss reverberated through her as his warm breath fanned her cheek.

"No buts. Be brave. Be spontaneous. Show me your clinic."

Be brave. Spontaneous. Warning bells went off in her head. She couldn't be spontaneous, adventurous. It never ended up well. She'd end up…oh, but he smelled so good; even the faint chlorine scent stirred her libido.

A loud scratching sounded from the front door. Allison recognized it easily.

"Ping's here. He must have followed me. I'll be right back." Grasping onto the excuse, she stepped away from him and fled.

Opening the door, she looked down at the dog. Dressed in a blue-and-hot-pink knitted tank top and matching booties, with a collar that sported at least three bells, Ping looked like a refugee from a muscle beach. Allison grinned down at him.

"Did you want me, boy? You should go home."

Ping barely spared her a glance as he dashed by her and into the bedroom. A few short barks followed.

Allison rushed after him. What now? Jay and Ping had been getting along at the pool. Had the dog reverted back to his normal attitude toward Jay?

Nope. Sitting on the bed with Ping next to him, Jay had removed the tank top and matching booties. He talked in low tones.

"There you go, pal. You look better now. I don't have a clue what to do about that collar, though. You need to wear your tags, but you also need your masculine pride," Jay studied the offending thing for a moment. Its bright blue color actually made Ping's flaxen mane exhibit a bluish tint. Allison watched the pair as the dog cocked his head at Jay, who smiled in triumph. "I have it! Stay there, buddy. I'll be right back." Standing carefully, Jay left the bedroom, heading toward the bathroom.

Allison moved out of his way as he hobbled past, holding back the impulse to smell him as he went by. Man scent, the ultimate turn-on.

He returned a moment later, dangling a chain bracelet from his fingers. "I think this will do. Very macho." Allison recognized the LAPD emblem dangling from it.

Removing Ping's collar, he transferred the tags from it to the bracelet, then slipped it over Ping's head. He adjusted the fit, patting the dog companionably. "Much better."

Ping, for his part very patient with the entire procedure, thanked Jay with a lick and a wag of his tail. He then lay down on the bed, panting contently.

"Birdie's not going to be very happy with you," Allison warned Jay.

"I look at it this way. Birdie hasn't bitten me, humped my leg, torn up my knee and practically drowned me. I'd rather have her angry at me than him."

Laughing, Allison acceded. "You have a point there."

He smiled at her as he ruffled Ping's crest. "So, are we going?"

Allison returned the smile. Getting injured seemed to have improved Jay's mood. "It's a long drive and you hate my car."

Jay's smile fell flat. "Oh, yeah, you have that torture chamber. Forgot about that. My truck's still at the station."

"We could go get it," she offered. "Paige isn't working today; maybe she'd drive it back for you."

He shook his head. "The truck wouldn't give me much more room. It's an old beater with a bench seat."

Allison bit her lip; he really wanted to go. She had her excuse to back out now, to give herself time to get her raging hormones under control.

Jay shrugged. "Well, it was an idea. Not a great one obviously." He reached for the book that Allison had set on the nightstand. His ruined copy of the novel now occupied a garbage can. "I can take advantage of my down time and read the rest of this. Or maybe catch a movie."

"I could go rent you one, if you like."

He shook his head. "Thanks, but I didn't bring my VCR. And usually there's an old Humphrey Bogart movie on that I can enjoy."

Allison gasped. "Jay, I have an entire collection of Bogey. I love him. I'll bring over my VCR and hook you up."

Jay grinned, as if she'd just offered him heaven. "That's an offer I can't refuse." He bent his sore knee slightly, almost succeeding in hiding his frustration. She could tell that the book, and even the offer of movies, didn't make up for his lost mobility. But it was the best that she could do.

"I'll be right back." Glancing down at Ping, she said, "Come on. You know Birdie'll be looking for you."

Reluctantly, the dog hopped down. Allison smiled at Jay one more time; he grinned back as he settled down with his book, injured leg, sans the still-wet brace, stretched out carefully in front of him.

She left the apartment, Ping preceding her just in time for Birdie to spot him. A black muumuu covered in red cherries made Birdie hard to overlook.

"Ping! There you are! I've been looking everywhere! You naughty boy! And where's your T-shirt?"

Picking up her pet, she studied the bracelet about his neck. Her mouth tightened.

"A cheap chain? Jay should ask before he strips my dog."

Allison found herself defending Jay, as if was her job to do so. "I think it's a guy thing, Birdie. They're actually getting along great. Hopefully that'll be an end to the 'Ping and Jay' incidents."

Birdie's face brightened. "That would be good. People are starting to avoid poor Ping, thinking this is all his fault. That bothers him; he's such a social animal."

Allison didn't know how to answer that. How Birdie could miss the reactions of others to Ping, she didn't know. Instead, she said, "I think I'd let him get away with this one little thing. But the collar,,, Maybe you can find Ping something that Jay would approve of. He probably wants that back. That's his LAPD ID bracelet."

"It is?" Stunned, Birdie studied it again. "Oh, it must mean a great deal to him, and he let Ping wear it." She glanced at Jay's door. "Maybe I misjudged him."

"Maybe we both did." She didn't respond to Birdie's wordless question on her face, instead asking, "Would you mind if I borrowed your car?"

Chapter Thirteen

His leg stretched out comfortably in front of him, Jay leaned back in the plush leather seats of Birdie's Toyota Avalon. *Much better than Allison's little Miata,* he mused. And it was a good sign that Allison had borrowed it to take him to see the clinic. Yes, a good sign that they could keep this truce going. He liked being at peace with her. He grinned as he added to himself that his crotch area appreciated the truce as well. He'd never been so 'chilled' in his life.

He felt lighter, more buoyant somehow, with her. That down, angry feeling that had filled him since the scandal had broken and he'd been exiled seemed to be part of his past now. Strange, really. Being injured should have made it worse, but somehow he couldn't think of anywhere he'd rather be than here, heading toward this mysterious clinic and finding out more about Allison Leavitt and what made her tick.

Of course, he'd rather be in her bed. But he dismissed that thought. Trying to further their intimate relationship was what had earned him the ice bath in the first place. He didn't plan on going there again anytime soon.

Her animated love for her volunteer work impressed the hell out of him. How compassionate and caring she'd turned out to be, and with that deep intelligence she exuded, he couldn't help but admire her.

The clinic, she'd told him, was situated on the Spokane River, with a gorgeous view over the water. Considering the price of waterfront property, he'd been surprised, but she'd told him that the owners of an abandoned private hospital had been touched at the proposed usage of the property and had sold it to them very cheaply, taking the 'loss' as a tax break. The view would go a great deal toward helping the patients lift their spirits.

They reached the river, and Jay rolled down his window, wanting to enjoy a breath of fresh air. It had nothing to do with Allison's raspberry scent reminding him that they were man and woman, alone. Nope. He only wanted to relish that intoxicating, outdoorsy, woody odor that reminded him that life didn't revolve solely around big cities, loud cars and people.

The view astounded him—deep blue water surrounded by majestic pines that he figured outdated him by decades.

"Isn't this a bit far from a hospital?" he asked. "I thought the point of something like this is to get to the patient in minutes."

Allison nodded. "Part of our operation is at the main hospital downtown. We'll have a small clinic there, staffed with doctors and nurses specially trained to deal with spinal injuries. This clinic can handle immediate care as well, along with long-term rehabilitation, counseling, learning new life skills, things like that. And it's really not that far from the hospital. It's about a mile away. Takes about two minutes to get here, and it's easily accessible. We even have a helipad."

The clinic came into view. The low-slung brick building didn't seem very large, but Jay knew that looks could definitely be deceiving.

Allison had done that, coming across, at first, as a flighty, empty person. He knew better now. He also had discerned that she didn't have a deceptive bone in her body. Allison couldn't keep secrets or stop her true self from bubbling out. And what he saw definitely attracted him. It wasn't just her looks, which would blow away any guy. No, her personality appealed to him as much as the physical package did.

He wanted to grasp her hand and feel that burst of electricity that always came with touching her. But she'd seemed nervous since showing up at his apartment. He didn't want to press her, so he rested his hands on his thighs, trying not to dwell how she'd felt against him last night.

🐈 🐈 🐈

Allison glanced at Jay's profile, careful not to be obvious. He seemed very relaxed, much more so than when she'd first met him. Made him seem more approachable. And his laugh came more frequently; she liked that.

Given her earlier attack of libido, she didn't know if that was a good thing. Her hormones were under control now, as long as she kept her distance.

She was positive, though, that she could smell his aftershave in the slight breeze that swept over him on its way to her.

They stood on the back deck of the clinic. Through the dense trees, they could glimpse a few other buildings, but it still felt isolated. They'd arrived when most of the contractors were out to lunch. That gave her a reprieve, since she knew that by the way the others treated her, Jay would realize she did more around here than paint walls and stock supplies.

Jay sucked in a deep breath. "The river is impressive. I can see how this is going to help the patients here." He slanted a carefree grin at her, and his boyishness fluttered her pulse just as easily as if he'd touched her.

She jerked as her stomach tightened in response. No, she couldn't get aroused now. She'd done so good the last hour or so. She'd almost forgotten how sexy he was, how addictive his smile could be, how it felt to be held by him.

Almost. They were alone out here, free from prying eyes. He could kiss her, hold her and nobody would be the wiser.

She realized she stared at him, taking in the long lashes and how his eyes echoed the blue of the sky and the river when he turned to her and captured her gaze with his own. He could sense her mood and passion flared on his face.

"Allie…"

She couldn't turn away from him, couldn't pull free from the spell he wove about her as he reached for her. His hand skimmed her cheek on its way to cup the back of her head and pull her close.

She gave no resistance, although a whimper escaped when he paused, his mouth nearly touching hers.

"I'm afraid to kiss you," he whispered.

"Why?" The word was merely a breath against his mouth, but he understood.

"Because I don't know if I can stop."

His words propelled her forward—she didn't want him to stop. Not now. Not ever. She pressed her body against his and caught his mouth against her own. His mouth crushed hers, demanding a response, demanding her passion, her fervor.

She gladly gave it to him. Desire burst in her chest; she couldn't get close enough, feel him strongly enough. All her senses were heightened; she could feel the entire length of him pressed against her, his arousal obvious.

She moaned as his lips traveled down to the base of her throat, nipping lightly at the sensitive pulse point there. She arched against him, loving the feel of his rough skin against her.

His hot breath fanned her burning flesh as his mouth traveled down to the neckline of her tank top, tasting the swell of the upper curve of her breast. His hands traveled up and down her back, transferring heat and need in their wake. They skimmed over her buttocks and she longed for him to cup her bottom, pulling her closer, molding her against him.

His mouth stopped where the fabric began. Allison groaned her impatience; she wanted more. She wanted to feel his mouth on her breast, suckling her nipple, traveling lower, lower still…

Her hands went to the hem of her tank top, meaning to jerk it up and off, giving him free access to her. But his hands covered hers, stopping her.

"Someone might see," he growled through his harsh breathing. "Allison—we're on the deck."

"Oh." She didn't care. Personally, people needed to lighten up. Shuddering with the strength of her emotions, she leaned her forehead against his shoulder. If she responded this wildly with a mere kiss, what would happen if they ever got the chance to go further?

🐈 🐈 🐈

Jay bundled her into his arms, holding her tenderly as she trembled. He listened to her breathing gradually come under control. He stroked her back soothingly as someone might a child, even though she didn't feel like a child to him; the lust that raged through him didn't let him even pretend their relationship could be platonic.

Lifting her face, she gazed at him. "Seems you don't hurt too much now."

Chuckling, he kissed her forehead. "Funny what you can forget about with the right distraction."

Her face lit with pleasure. "I'm glad I'm at least distracting."

He moaned at her innocence. "If only you knew!"

Laughing, she rocked her pelvis up against his throbbing arousal. "I do know, believe me."

Groaning, he eased away from her. Not so naive, after all. If she did that one more time, to hell with the neighbors!

Time to talk to her about wanting to date her. She seemed very receptive to him right now. "Allison..."

Voices carried over to them as the front door swept open. Allison stepped swiftly away from him, running her hands down her shirt. Jay watched her retreat with regret. For an instant, he'd felt one with her. He'd sensed that they'd connected, in more than just a physical way.

The workers, sharing a private joke, were laughing when they finally noticed Allison and Jay. One of them smiled in greeting and crossed over to them.

"Allison," he exclaimed. "I didn't expect you until later."

"I decided to bring a friend," she said. She plastered on a smile. She knew Jeff bristled with pride over their accomplishments. She needed to keep him from spilling the beans—now wasn't the time to discuss her past stupidities, not when she and Jay were getting along so well. "He wanted to see the clinic. I thought maybe Marcie could give him a tour while you and I talk." Marcie, the head nurse, wouldn't give Allison away. A closed-mouth woman, she'd tell Jay the bare facts about the clinic, and little more. Hopefully, this would protect Allison from too many questions from Jay.

She introduced the two men; Jay shook the hand offered to him. "Jeff is the administrator here," Allison said. "He's the one who keeps this place going."

Jeff, a small wiry man, grinned. "Thanks, but Allison here's the real inspiration. She—"

"Oh, there's Marcie!" In a panic, wanting to hush Jeff up, Allison waved the large, buxom, middle-aged woman over. "Marcie, do you think you could give Jay a tour of the place? He hurt his knee a few days ago, and isn't wearing his brace, so you might want to go slow."

Marcie's eyes swept up and down Jay, no doubt taking in his tousled hair, then traveled up Allison's form. Allison's cheeks warmed up dramatically at the telling lift of Marcie's brows. "Well, I can see you gave him a thorough tour of the deck, so maybe we'll start with the weight room." Waving an arm, she gestured at Jay to follow her. With a grin, he ambled after the woman, his hand momentarily squeezing Allison's upper arm as he passed. Her skin missed his touch when he was gone.

"Did I say something wrong?" Jeff asked.

"No, but Jay thinks I only volunteer here. I'm a bit reluctant to tell him everything."

"You shouldn't be, Allison. You should be proud of the work you do here."

"I am, but…" *But I don't want to tell him of my crime, not until I'm ready.* "This isn't about me, Jeff. This is about helping people who need it."

Apparently today, Allison couldn't fool anyone. "You can't keep hiding from the guilt you feel," Jeff said. "I don't know what caused it, but someday you're going to have to deal with it."

Allison didn't reply, but she felt culpable for more than the accident. By not telling Jay of her involvement here, and not revealing to him his resemblance to her newest cover art, Allison had done something she'd accused Nick of—basing a relationship on falsehood.

The ride home passed pleasantly. Allison popped in a CD of old Beatles hits, and both of them laughingly sang off-key to their favorite tunes.

"I'm impressed, Allie," Jay said. "That clinic's going to be state of the art. I can see why you're so enthused over it."

Luckily, it seemed that Allison's full involvement in the clinic remained hidden. She'd gotten all the papers she'd needed to review done well before Jay returned from his tour. He had looked happy, but very tired.

"Thanks," she said, wishing she didn't feel so guilty. Wasn't she stealing this time with him? How would he react when he discovered that she'd been less than honest with him?

Chapter Fourteen

When they arrived home, Allison took one look at Jay and recognized that he was drained. The excursion, although fun, had exhausted him. Reluctantly, she suggested a nap to him and quelled a twinge of disappointment when he accepted.

A few minutes later, Allison stood in front of her computer, contemplating a long writing session, yet thinking of where she could be instead. With a sigh, she reached for the envelope containing the artist rendering of Ben Stark. She pulled it out and propped it up. It did resemble Jay, but only on the outside.

She could never have imagined anyone like Jay. Perhaps she'd fantasized about someone like him, but in her daydreams, she'd missed the facets and nuances that Jay possessed. He could be strong and professional when necessary, yet still show a little dog a great kindness by removing a hated shirt. He could growl one minute and give her waves of immense passion the next. Yes, she'd never again mistake him for a creation on paper, that was for sure.

She sat down and powered up the computer. Time to shake up Ben Stark's world. Soon she'd eliminate his partner, Emily, then bring back the love of his life. The book was going to be the best thing she'd ever written. And the hardest. She'd miss Emily; she'd become one of her best characters.

Opening up the file of her latest chapter, Allison settled down to the task at hand, but her eyes wandered from time to time to the artwork that so resembled the man she wanted with her.

The hours flew by as she laid down her plot, added rich details, twisted things about. She fell into the story as she wove intrigue about Ben and Emily and their quest to find Molly's killer.

Darkness had fallen when she finally sat back, exhausted but satisfied. Her shoulders ached and she knew her butt was numb, but she'd accomplished a lot, and if she did say so herself, she'd created her finest effort to date. The scene where Ben had tried to explain to Emily the feelings he harbored for his missing love… *Yes*, she thought. *That was inspired!*

And, she admitted, it was fueled by her wish that Jay sat by her, waiting patiently for her to finish and turn to him for some inspiring lovemaking.

After saving her file to both the hard drive and a CD, she shut down the computer. Allison turned off the desk light just as she caught movement out of the corner of her eye. With a shriek, she whirled in her chair, preparing to confront her intruder.

And found Jay standing in her open French doors.

"You really need to keep this locked," he told her, his tone of affection softening his words. "After all, didn't your killer come through these very doors?"

Allison glanced guiltily at the Ben Stark painting, but it blended into the darkness and couldn't be seen. However, if he drew closer, he'd be sure to notice it. She needed to bring it up in her own time; she still hadn't heard from her publisher about why this painting looked like Jay.

Torpedoing out of her chair, anxious to shift his focus from the computer area, she rushed to him. "You startled me! I thought you were napping. I'll start locking it. I don't think I can take another shock walking through that door."

"Allie!" Laughing his surprise, he stopped her headlong progress by gripping her shoulders. "I woke up hours ago and wondered where you were. You've definitely got a lot of energy tonight."

The painting burned a hole through the back of her head. "I do, don't I? Boy, it's hot tonight. I could use a swim." Too late, she remembered his knee. "Can you swim? If not, we could—"

"You haven't been drinking coffee, have you? You're practically bouncing off the walls."

"No." She smiled brightly at him while maneuvering herself away from the desk. "Don't touch the stuff. Could you imagine me on caffeine?" *Stop it, Allison,* she berated herself. Why, any second now she'd start the fish-face thing!

Chuckling, his fingers slid down her arms to grip her hands. "I'm afraid to go there." Grinning down at her, he added, "The doctor told me that swimming would be good for my knee. How about I go change and I'll meet you poolside?"

The thought of Jay in nothing but swim trunks raised her blood level measurably. *You wanted an affair with him,* she reminded herself. *Might as well get a sneak preview.*

But did she really want a fling with him? She'd be risking heartbreak—she couldn't see herself making love to him and not loving him.

But what if she did walk away in the end? What would she have left? Memories to be cherished and savored? Or emptiness and regret?

She pushed the depressing thoughts away, and did something bold—she stepped into the unknown.

"Sounds like fun," she replied brightly. "It'll take just a few minutes to change."

"Great."

Her exuberance must have struck a nerve in him, because he looked at her strangely. "What?"

"Nothing," grinning, he shuffled through the French door. "See you in a few."

Breathing a sigh of relief, Allison locked the door behind him and then rushed toward her bedroom. Why had she suggested swimming? All she had were some ancient, one-piece suits! Why couldn't she own just one sexy thing?

🐾 🐾 🐾

In the end, she wore a plain, black, one-piece suit covered by a mesh black shirt that reached the middle of her thighs. She'd remembered why she didn't own anything sexy: she needed to cover the scars on her back.

The fall, and two subsequent surgeries, had left her with unsightly reminders of her foolishness. She'd learned from past experience that guys didn't find them conducive to amorous thoughts. She doubted Jay would be any different.

But maybe something with a bit of cleavage would be nice, she reasoned. Nothing wrong with her front side. Maybe she'd do some shopping. Soon. Thinking of Jay's eyes lighting up with admiration, she added: *Very soon.*

She slipped a pair of sandals on her feet, grabbed a couple of towels and headed out to the pool. Moonlight sparkled on the water as she approached; nobody waited for her. She tossed the towels on a nearby lounge chair, pulled the ponytail holder out of her hair and left it sitting on the towels. Shaking her hair loose, she stared out at the pool for a moment. Then, with a whoop and a run, she dove into the water.

It was cool and refreshing against her skin and supported her as she swam the length of the pool beneath its surface. She rejoiced in the stretch and pull of her muscles as her body sliced through the water. Looking up, she could see a pair of long muscled legs standing at the shallow end of the pool, only a few feet ahead of her.

Jay. Her heart leapt at his presence. Breaking through the water's surface, she sucked in a deep breath, then grinned up at him.

Only he wasn't alone. Taffy stood by him, ultra-sexy in a red, crocheted bikini that barely contained her abundant breasts. She talked to Jay in low whispers. Glancing at Allison, she giggled.

"When you're ready for a real woman, call me," she purred as she walked off.

"Like that would be you," Allison muttered.

Jay leaned down toward her. "I heard that."

"Good," she smiled up at him, enjoying the carefree grin he gave her. Much, much better than the grumpy man she'd met a few days ago. "What did she want?"

"To thank me, actually. Which surprised me. Told me that she'd been doing some thinking after I tore into her, and that she needed to restructure her life so that she could be independent without having to rely on men."

"Use men, you mean," Allison stared after the woman, who'd disappeared from her sight. "You think she meant it?" She found it hard to believe that Taffy the Man-Eater would ever change her spots.

Jay paused, giving her question some thought. "I think she did. At least she does right now. Whether or not she follows through remains to be seen. But she did do something nice—she decided to skip her swim and let us have some privacy."

Allison scowled, "She couldn't resist one last dig at me."

Jay sat down at the pool edge, carefully adjusting his badly bruised and braceless knee in front of him. "I think you bother her. She can understand Paige, who's looking for love, who enjoys dressing up and who likes the finer things in life. She can probably even understand Birdie. I know I don't." He grinned and Allison felt herself respond to the warmth she found there. "But you. You're an enigma to her. A beautiful woman who depends on her brains instead of her looks. She's only counted on the lust of men to get forward in life. You, though— you lean on yourself. You're everything she thinks she can never be. How can you expect her not to take jabs at you?"

Funny—placing herself in Taffy's shoes had never occurred to her. But she didn't hold much faith in the blonde's sudden turn-around. "I guess time will tell what she does."

"Yeah." Jay lowered himself slowly in the water and swam a few feet.

"How's it feel?"

"Strange. Like it's not quite connected."

"Do you want to hang off the edge for a while?"

"That sounds like a plan," Jay replied.

Allison couldn't help but admire his firm, muscled chest. With him being a cop, she knew that he'd take good care of himself. She'd expected him to be fit. What she hadn't expected was her reaction to him.

After a few minutes, he seemed to grow more comfortable with his injury. They went around the pool slowly to accommodate his sore knee. They'd made a few laps, talking quietly and sharing soft laughter when Paige and Pearce came out from the building and crossed over to them.

Pearce's arm encircled Paige's waist; Allison could tell that they'd worked their problems out. Her friend glowed with happiness as she gazed at Pearce with loving eyes. She'd never seen her so taken with a man.

"Al!" Paige's smile seemed too large for her to contain. "I wanted to thank you for your help. Without you and Jay I wouldn't have had the courage to give Pearce a call. I'd still be trying to figure out how to get over him instead of being with him now." She smiled up at him; their gazes devoured each other. Their looks were so hot and intimate that Allison felt uncomfortable watching. "He explained about Taffy, how she'd come on to him, how he'd turned her down. I believe him now. Before, I'd been too hurt and stubborn to listen."

"Jay," Pearce frowned at his partner. "Paige told me what you said to her. I wanted to thank you." Allison could see his discomfort; apparently the two men were still not at peace with each other. Pearce having to thank Jay probably didn't sit well with either man.

"Hey," Jay protested. "If I hadn't done that, she'd never have gone away!"

Pearce laughed as Paige squawked her protest at Jay. "You've got a point there, pal. She can be very persistent when her mind's set on something."

Paige rolled her eyes. "Why I ever thought I needed a man in my life, I'll never know! All he does is tease me, Al. It's been awful, I tell you." But her eyes told a different story; that with Pearce she'd found a new depth of happiness.

For the first time in a long time, Allison wanted someone like that in her life: someone to lean on, to touch, hold and share things with. She didn't dare look at Jay. She feared that everything she felt would show on her face. How would he react?

"I'm glad you two got together," she said. "Maybe we should celebrate?"

"That sounds like fun!" Paige exclaimed. "We're on our way to a movie right now, but how about if we meet for breakfast?"

"At Pancake Heaven?" Allison eyed her friend expectantly. She loved that restaurant; Paige did too, but she enjoyed pretending that it was a sacrifice to go with Allison there so frequently.

Paige laughed. "You really need to find some new restaurants, Al. We could try brunch at the new hotel downtown," she said hopefully.

"Since this is your celebration, Paige," Jay said. "Perhaps we should let you choose the place."

"You know, I'm really starting to like you," Paige chortled through her laughter as Allison mock-pouted.

Pearce glanced at his watch and smiled apologetically at the others. "Babe, if we're going to make the movie, we need to leave now." He looked at Allison and Jay. "How about if we meet you at the hotel tomorrow at ten?"

"Sounds good," Jay said.

"By the way, we caught that guy earlier today, and he gave us some great leads to work with. We figure we'll have the case wrapped up soon."

"That's great," Jay said. "Thanks for letting me know."

The other couple departed. Allison watched them wistfully. She'd love to have something long-term and permanent like that, but she didn't want to pay the price. She'd have to give up her freedom, her peace of mind, and probably her self-esteem when yet another man used her.

Glancing at Jay, she felt ashamed. She didn't know him that well yet, but from everything she'd seen, she didn't think he'd ever treat a woman in that way. So why did she have to suspect the worst of him?

Because you've never met a man who didn't want you for your money, she reminded herself. But did that mean that she had to paint Jay with the same brush? Or could she learn to trust him?

"Hey," Jay asked softly. "Where'd you disappear to just now?"

In the soft light that bathed the water, he looked incredibly handsome. Shivers of desire coiled in her, but confusion stopped her. What should she do? Did she want to be with him until he left for L.A., or did she want to protect herself from the pain she'd feel when he departed?

She decided to take a chance. It felt like stepping into an abyss, not knowing if anyone would catch her. Not knowing how far she'd fall.

"I was thinking about you," she admitted, her voice a hoarse whisper. "I was trying to decide if I should let this happen, or protect myself and walk away."

If Jay felt surprised, his face didn't show it. His hand reached out and a finger stroked her cheek tenderly. "If you chose to walk away, I'd always wonder what we've missed. I've never felt so attracted to a woman before. You reach me on so many levels. I have to admit I'd be lying if I said I wasn't afraid." His thumb stroked her bottom lip, firming its touch when her mouth trembled.

"Allie," he whispered, his breath caressing her skin as he leaned closer. "What if this is it? What if this is our best chance to find the happiness we're meant to have? Wouldn't it be tragic if we didn't try, out of fear?"

Allison's trembling increased as his words hit home. What if, by protecting herself, she remained empty for the rest of her life? Did she really want to be alone, with no one to share her triumphs and failures?

Looking into Jay's eyes, the answer reverberated through her. "I don't think I could live with that," she admitted. "I don't want to walk away."

He responded by sweeping her into his arms, his mouth finding hers with a passion she'd never experienced. If she'd had any reason to doubt his sincerity before, the depths of his feelings that he revealed in that kiss wiped them all away. Desire, caring, tenderness—they were all there in the taste, touch and feel of him.

Her arms wrapped tightly around him as she kissed him back, conveying her need for him clearly. The warm water buoyed them, intensifying the moment. All that kept them from sinking was Jay's hand on the edge of the pool; Allison would've gladly drowned to enjoy even one more second in his arms.

His free hand slipped under her mesh shirt and stroked her back, pulling her even closer, molding her against him. She moaned at the contact; Jay responded by deepening the kiss. He tasted of chlorine and passion - an intoxicating mix she had to have.

His fingers skimmed over her scars, a twisted pattern of hardened skin. She felt his hands stop and gently probe his discovery.

She pulled away from him as he looked at her in confusion. "Allie? What happened?"

She expected to feel shame and remnants of the pain that had caused the scars. But at the softness of his gaze, instead she felt compelled to share with him.

"In my younger years, I was quite a dare devil. Bet you never would've guessed that!" Allison laughed to hide her nervousness. "I loved climbing over the rock formations at Minnehaha Park and one day, this group of teenagers watched me."

She told him of the boy, unknown to her, who'd followed her up the cliff, of him freezing halfway up and her attempt to rescue him. Allison shook with the strength of her memories. Jay stroked her arm and she found comfort in his touch.

"He panicked and pushed me away, then reached for a finger hold. But he missed and started to fall. Somehow I got hold of him. I'm not sure why it happened; either in my haste to get to him, I didn't hook the harness right, or the force of catching him damaged the equipment, but something gave way and we fell over twenty feet. He wasn't wearing a helmet; I knew if he landed first he'd be dead. So I twisted in midair. I hit first."

Jay hissed. "How badly were you injured?"

Allison grimaced. "Pretty bad. I broke my back, my pelvis and a bunch of other bones. Luckily, my helmet took the brunt of my fall, so I didn't have a head injury. The boy got off a bit luckier. Broken ribs, broken leg, minor concussion. He had a much shorter hospital stay than I did. I spent nearly a year there and at a rehab center. The scars are from two surgeries to repair the damage."

She didn't tell him the rest. The visit from the boy's mother, accusing her of causing his accident by setting a 'bad example.' Those terrifying weeks when she'd thought she'd never walk, let alone run, again. Then meeting Birdie and finally, that first step. She'd never slowed down since. But she'd learned a lesson: she didn't take unnecessary risks anymore.

"Hence the desire to help out at the rehab center. You want to give back some of what was given you."

Allison nodded. "Yes."

"You had a rough time of it," he said. "But it looks like you've recovered well. How's the boy?"

"I'm not sure," she said. "I didn't keep in touch with him." She gazed into the water; she'd talked enough about it. She didn't want to tell him she'd never been allowed to visit the boy. So she distracted Jay instead.

"I'm sure, being a big-time cop," she teased him, "That you have some scars with good stories of their own."

Jay smiled wickedly, tossing his arms open. "Would you like to find out?"

With a laugh she moved back into his arms; this time she wouldn't let anything stop them, especially bad memories.

"Would you get angry with me if I suggested we take this inside?" His words tickled her skin as his mouth traveled to the base of her throat, inflaming her even further.

"I think…" She moaned her reply. "That would be the prudent thing to do."

Grasping his hand, she led him to the pool stairs as her fingers clung tightly to him. She didn't want to lose contact with him; his warmth gave her strength.

Once out of the pool, Jay took command. Wrapping one arm about her, he picked up the towels. He enfolded her in the softness of one while slinging the other about his neck. Then he led her to his place. The searing look in his eyes left her in no doubt of the depth of his need for her.

Closing the door behind them, Jay took her in his arms, reintroducing her to the heat he generated with his kisses.

"I'd carry you into the bedroom," he laughed against her mouth. "But that could be a disaster for both of us."

"I think I can manage to walk that far," she replied, humor bubbling up through the passion. Clinging to each other, unwilling to break contact, they made the short journey to the bedroom.

As he laid her down on his rumpled bed, Allison knew this was where she belonged. Opening her arms to him, she welcomed him with all the love that bloomed inside her.

Chapter Fifteen

Jay's heart clenched as he lay down beside Allison. She looked so stunning in the filtered light that cascaded through the window. He'd never imagined a woman could be as beautiful or enticing as his Allie was at that very moment.

He desired nothing more than to make love to her, to feel a part of her in every sense of the word. But he wanted more than this one moment with her; he wanted her to become an important piece of his world. Would becoming intimate with her right now lose him that opportunity?

He hesitated, uncertain if he should take the chance. He knew now that his future belonged with this woman. But he also knew from the uncertainty she tried to hide from him that she still held part of herself back.

"Jay," she moaned, her arms tugging at him. She arched toward him. "Don't torture me like this. I need you."

Her entreaty tore away his last resolve. If this was a mistake, he'd deal with the consequences later. Right now, all he could think of was his beautiful Allie. She filled his senses, stripped away all reasoning and logical thought and replaced it with the overwhelming need of being with her.

He removed her mesh cover-up, then pulled the straps of her swimsuit down, exposing the pale breasts he'd fantasized about. They

Stacia Wolf

were full and perfect and inflamed him even further. Yet still, he hesitated.

"Allie, are you sure this is what you want?" He sucked in a ragged breath as he waited for her answer. "Because if you're not sure, we need to stop now."

"I don't want to stop," she whispered. "I need you." Her passionate tones left him in no doubt of her sincerity.

He needed no other encouragement. His mouth found one beckoning nipple; savoring her taste, her feel, her incredible softness, he pressed himself into her. He removed her wet swimsuit fully, savoring the sight of her as he did so. Curvy, with a pale skin that complemented her ginger curls, she embodied his perfect vision of a woman.

She exhibited a boldness he hadn't expected as her fingers found the top of his swim trunks, tugging them down and exposing him to her searching hands. She touched his arousal, the warmth of her skin provoking him. It was too much; he pulled her hand away.

"No, don't," he rasped. "I want this to last. If you do that again I can guarantee it won't."

She laughed, the knowledge of her power over him blatant in her eyes. "Then we'd just have to start all over again, wouldn't we?"

With a growl, he nipped at her shoulder, eliciting a laughing shriek of protest from her. "Woman, you're driving me crazy," he said. "I'm not sure it's a good thing."

Her laughter stroked him as her fingers gripped his shoulders, pulling him down into the softness of her breasts. Her amusement died as his hand stroked her hip, then traveled to the juncture of her legs. His arousal laid heavy against her as his fingers touched her, exploring her. She arched against him, demanding more.

Capturing her mouth with his, he felt himself being lost in the wonder that was Allison.

His fingers invaded Allison, teasing her with their rhythm as she pressed against his hand, demanding him to deepen the touch. She had never been subject to such burning need; her mind exploded with the overwhelming sensations her body experienced. She arched against him. The heat of his skin felt perfect, right, against her hardened nipples. She leaned back, silently begging him to suckle her. As if reading her mind, he obligingly covered one aching nub with his mouth.

His tongue teased the nipple, roughing it and rolling it before he sucked it between his lips. She moaned, feeling herself moisten against his fingers, which remained deep inside her. Her hips rocked against him, matching the movements of his hand. Her hands explored his back, hungering for the feel of his skin and the hard, smooth muscles she discovered. Her fingers buried themselves in his silky smooth, golden-blond hair.

His finger plunged into her as his thumb continued a rhythm that drove her closer to the edge. She couldn't stand anymore of it. Writhing against him, she maneuvered herself until the tip of his manhood touched her wetness. She thrust herself toward him, moaning as he entered her.

Cupping her buttocks with his hands, he thrust into her, sliding deeper into her sleek warmth. Her legs wrapped around him as she bucked beneath him, intensifying the pressure on her over-sensitized flesh. Tilting her pelvis, she invited him deeper into her as she matched his rhythm.

Nothing existed anymore; only Jay and his body. The feel of what he did to her overrode everything but this exact moment. Their personal body scents mingled, becoming unique and wildly erotic. She clenched around him, felt him swell in response and pump deeper and deeper into her. Clutching his buttocks, she moved wildly beneath him, suddenly realizing that she hovered on the brink. She held onto that impossible moment for as long as she could—it contained healing for her, erased self-doubt and brought about wonder that she'd reached this.

One more thrust and she shattered.

She spun out of control and clung to him tightly. Waves of passion blinded her. She muffled her groans in his shoulder as she relished this, her impossible orgasm. She felt him engorge, then release inside her.

She kissed his shoulder and listened to his ragged breathing as she fought to control her own. He tasted salty and male, felt like sex and comfort. And belonging.

He wrapped his arms about her and laughed, a gentle, satisfied sound that echoed in her heart. He kissed the top of her head, and she snuggled into his chest, feeling pretty darn pleased with herself.

"So," he growled in her ear. "Do you still think that sex is disappointing?"

She kissed his chest, loving the feel of his hair-roughen skin under her lips. "I think that it'll get better," she said, unable to contain a giggle. "But we need a lot of practice."

🐾 🐾 🐾

"Allie," the voice rumbled in her ear. "C'mon, babe, you need to wake up. We overslept; it's after nine."

"Oh, my gosh! We have to meet Paige and Pearce at ten!" Catapulting from bed, Allison hunted for her swimsuit and found it in a damp pile. Wrinkling her nose in distaste, she started to pull it on.

"Here." Jay held out a white terrycloth bathrobe he grabbed from the bathroom as he stood before her in his full glory. Allison sucked in a tortured breath as she tried to ignore his nudity. She couldn't linger over him or she'd be tempted to repeat last night.

They'd 'practiced' several times through the night, each time learning new ways to please each other. She'd never felt so fulfilled, so in tune with anyone as she did with him. She'd fallen asleep in his arms, feeling safe and cherished for the first time in her adult life.

She slipped her arms into the robe. "Thanks." Wrapping it about her, she snatched up her bathing suit and shirt and headed toward the door. "Meet you at my place in half an hour?"

One thing she had to say for waking up late—she didn't have any time to feel that morning awkwardness.

"Wait," Jay pulled her close, kissing her with a passion and longing that erupted a similar response in her. "And you'd better make it twenty minutes if we're going to be on time." He grinned mockingly as he gave her a gentle push, sending her on her way.

Wrapped in the warmth of Jay's lovemaking, Allison hummed as she made her way home. She danced through the French doors and into the bathroom, discarding the robe as she went. Swaying in front of the mirror, she noticed the faint love bite on her shoulder and…

"Ack!" She screamed at her reflection. She suddenly realized she'd broken the one rule she'd promised never to break again.

She'd gone to sleep with wet hair!

Her normally unruly curls were now all mangled wildly about her head; one side stood almost straight up for least four inches. She wailed in despair. Jay'd seen her like this!

Her wail died on her lips. He'd seen her like this, and he'd still wanted to kiss her! Either he'd hidden his blindness well or it hadn't mattered. Allison grinned at the last thought, then cried out one more time at the sight of her hair.

There was no way she could tame the tangled mess in two hours, let alone twenty minutes. It took her more than five to comb through the mass. Unfortunately, all that accomplished was to leave her with a frizzy pile flying about her head. Running her hands under the faucet, she combed them through her hair in an attempt to calm it down. She had no choice. There was no time to wash and dry it; that would take over a half hour alone, and she still needed to get dressed. Plugging in the curling iron, she rushed to the bedroom while it heated up.

A few minutes later, wearing a jade-green sundress and white, high-heeled sandals, Allison turned her attention once more to her hair. With swift movements, she curled and straightened her locks into some semblance of a hairstyle. Unfortunately, it resembled something one might see from the sixties. In quiet desperation, she hunted for a ponytail holder to corral the curls just as she heard Jay arrive.

"I'll be right out!" she called to him. No time to worry about the hair; quickly applying blush and lipstick, Allison left the bathroom. Her heart buoyed at the thought of kissing him again.

"Wow!" Jay gave a soft whistle as he saw her. "I like the hair." Pulling her into his arms, he gave her a swift kiss, one that sang with possession and joy.

Allison rolled her eyes at him. "Of course you'd like it," she told him with mock sarcasm. "Men love big hair."

Jay grinned evilly. "I see what you mean. We once raided a movie studio and one of the stars had hair just like that. What was the name of that movie? *Serena's Sex Secrets?* No, it was *Tammy's Titillating*—"

Laughing, Allison pushed at his chest, her face burning in embarrassment at being compared, even teasingly, to a porn movie. "Never mind!" She touched her hair self-consciously. "Does it look that bad?"

He smiled tenderly and kissed the tip of her nose. "It's lovely, baby. Are you ready to go?"

With a start, she realized she'd left her purse in the bedroom. "Hold on a second. I'll be right back."

As fast as her shoes would allow, Allison rushed into the bedroom and retrieved her purse. Returning to Jay, she found…

Him, holding the artwork for her next book. She'd left it propped up by her computer and had forgotten about it.

At his stiff posture and the tight look on his face, she could tell he wasn't amused. Panic tightened her throat; she'd never gotten the chance to tell him about it.

"I can explain," she blurted. "I didn't know—"

"This isn't me," he said, his voice laced with chilling anger. "The question is, is that what last night was all about?"

"I don't understand." His coldness scared her. She needed to touch him and bridge that. She reached out to him; he jerked away, leaving her with diminishing hope.

"What is this? What's it for?"

That wasn't the question she expected. "It's for my next cover. For my book."

His eyes never left the artwork. "You're published?"

Allison blinked. "You didn't know?" Although she never bragged about it, most of the inhabitants here knew. She'd have thought someone would have told him.

His silver eyes traveled to her face. They were devoid of the tenderness she realized she'd cherished, and now that it was gone, his gaze froze her to the core.

"Allison Leavitt. Al Leavitt. Paige even calls you Al. I've even read your books, and I never made the connection." He propped the art board back where he'd found it. "I'm pretty dense. You all must have laughed at me." He smiled, a bitter, twisted thing. "And here I thought you lived like this, with such bare surroundings, because you couldn't afford any better."

She shook her head. "I don't like clutter. And I never laughed at you."

His slight smile held no humor. "Damn, you're good. So I wonder, what fantasy were you living out? One that involved my brother? Or one with the hero you created?"

Allison stared at him in stunned confusion. "Your brother?"

Jay snorted. "You know, ten minutes ago, I would have believed that innocent look on your face. But if it was true, why didn't you tell me about this? The only answer I can come up with is that you had something to hide."

"I was trying to find out why it looks like you. My publisher hasn't called—"

"Allison, you know why it looks like me. Because the model looks like me. Again, why? Why am I here? It can't be a coincidence that I'm here, right when you plan a cover that finally reveals what Ben—that's his name, if I remember right— looks like to the world. What did you do, 'Al?' Call in some favors? I'm sure a famous author would find it no trouble at all to arrange a cop's transfer.

"All I can figure out is that it's a sick way for you to live out a fantasy. I'm starting to think that my brother doesn't interest you. So it must be to play out your little sexual fantasies with your dream man. You weren't sleeping with me last night, but with him." With a flick of disgust, he knocked over Ben's image flat on the computer desk.

"Here I felt trivial when I discovered my last lover really wanted my brother. Now I'm second fiddle to a paper man."

"No, Jay, it wasn't like that at all. I admit, at first I thought about it, your resemblance to Ben, but—"

"Save it, Al. I don't want to hear any more lies." His lips twisted in derision. "This explains things, though. I did wonder what an incredible woman like you could see in a mere cop."

He didn't spare her a glance as he stormed out.

Chapter Sixteen

"Al, did you forget about breakfast?" Paige's voice held more than a hint of impatience. Allison stifled a sob as she rolled over on her bed, clutching the phone to her ear.

"I don't think we're coming," she told Paige with a shaking voice. "Jay…Jay's not talking to me." She'd tried to find him and talk some reason into him, but he wouldn't answer the phone or his door.

Why hadn't she told him before? She could have made a joke out of it, made it a funny coincidence that they both could have laughed about. Instead, he probably thought her a stalker or a nutcase.

"What happened? When we saw you two last night, it looked like you were getting along great. In fact, I thought something romantic might be brewing."

"I thought so too, but he saw the book cover and… Paige, he went crazy! He thinks that either I was after his brother, which makes no sense, or that I was pretending he was Ben! Now he's gone and he won't talk to me." As she spoke, hot tears escaped, and she couldn't control the agony in her voice.

"Oh, honey. I'll be right there; just hang on."

"Paige, no, you don't have—" But Paige had hung up. Allison curled up on her bed, hugging a pillow to her chest as she let the tears flow.

Sure enough, a few minutes later, she heard a loud knock at the door. Pulling herself off the bed, she went to let Paige in.

Only it wasn't Paige standing there; it was Birdie. Along with Ping, of course, wearing a full regalia of bib shorts and a red T-shirt. A matching red collar complete with a fat silver bell encircled his neck.

"Paige told me. She can't get here for a little while and she didn't want you alone," Birdie said, her eyes filled with sympathy. Setting Ping down, she reached for her. "Oh, honey, I'm so sorry, but I'm here now. You'll be okay."

She bundled Allison into her arms. With a deep sob, Allison clung to her.

"You did something silly, didn't you?" Birdie asked. "You fell in love with him."

"No," she protested, but she knew Birdie spoke the truth. She loved Jay Cantrall, and now she faced a broken heart.

🐈 🐈 🐈

Jay tried to control his anger, but it kept boiling over every time he thought about her. He couldn't believe he'd been duped again. Of course, Allison Leavitt had her innocent act down pat.

He'd heard the phone ring a number of times, and the knocking at his door. But he had no desire to talk to Allison; not now and probably not ever.

All his life, he'd dealt with women preferring his more outgoing, charismatic brother over him. Most of the time it hadn't bothered him; in fact, it had rather amused him. But this time, like the last, he'd been taken totally by surprise. His emotions had been involved by the time he'd realized he'd been sucked in by a smooth operator. And this was even worse, because everything pointed to her not wanting him for his brother, but instead for his resemblance to a fictional character she'd created.

And he couldn't believe that in the time they'd spent together, she'd never told him who she really was. They'd made love, for God's sake! She didn't think that meant he should know she was a best-selling author?

The extent of her lies and omissions tore at him and he raged in frustration at his own stupidity. Forever the dupe. Always the last to know. At least, this time he'd be spared the front page scandal.

Restless and hating the confines of his apartment, Jay decided to take some affirmative action concerning his situation. Picking up the phone, he called his partner, Stan, and let him know that he'd be back in town as soon as it could be arranged. He then called his current captain to formally end his transfer to Spokane. The man didn't seem surprised and agreed immediately.

After the obligatory thank-you's and goodbyes, Jay hung up and waited for that feeling of satisfaction that came with resolving an issue. But it never materialized. Instead, he felt a sense of loss.

Once again, unbidden, the scene played over and over in his head. Walking into Allison's place, seeing the artwork of his brother propped by her computer, he'd known that her innocent act was just that: an act. Why she'd lied about it seemed unimportant right now. The fact she'd hid it told him the entire story. She wasn't to be trusted.

An insistent scratching sounded from the front door. Definitely not Allison. He recognized that 'knock.' Opening it, he found Ping looking up at him expectantly.

"Well, what are you waiting for? C'mon in." He stepped aside as the dog trotted in. He jumped on the couch, watching Jay hopefully.

"I take it you want a costume change again." Sitting down by the dog, Jay removed the outfit, except for the collar. He didn't have his bracelet back from Birdie yet, so he had nothing to use as a replacement. He shrugged at the dog apologetically.

"Best I can do, pal." Ping watched him for a moment, then, apparently realizing that Jay planned to do nothing more, he hopped off the couch and went to the door. Jay let him out, watching him trot down the hallway.

Shutting the door, he returned to the solitude he'd chosen. Somehow, it felt more empty than ever.

🐾 🐾 🐾

"That's ridiculous!" Paige spat out the words. "Why did he come to that conclusion?"

"I don't know." Sitting on her futon couch, Allison watched Paige pace back and forth, trying to make sense of what she'd told her. All Allison could think of was why she'd chosen now to take a risk. Especially with Jay.

Because you felt safe with him. Yes, she'd felt that, and much more. Stupid mistake for her to make. Brushing away a tear, she promised herself she'd never repeat such a ridiculous error.

Paige took notice of the tears, and sat down beside her. "I'm sorry, honey, I'm being a jerk. Here I am ranting and raving about what an ass Jay is, and I'm not taking care of you." She handed Allison a tissue, and smiled at her. "Would it help any for me to tell you that I'll gladly castrate him for you?"

Paige's ridiculous statement drew a laugh out of Allison. "No, I don't think that would help." She couldn't help a glimmer of mischief. "But it's a good thought."

Paige flashed an answering grin that a knock at the door interrupted.

"I'll get it," Paige said. "It's probably Birdie." The landlady had left a few minutes earlier to go look for Ping, who'd snuck out when Paige arrived.

Allison watched her open the door. She squelched the ridiculous hope that it would be Jay, coming to make up. At Paige's stiffened back, she could tell her visitor was unwanted.

"Taffy, what are you doing here?" Paige didn't make any effort to hide her hostility. After what the woman had put her through over Pearce, Allison didn't blame her.

"I didn't come here to talk to you," Taffy said, her voice sharp. "I want to talk to Allison. About Jay."

"Paige, it's all right. I don't mind talking to her." Wiping away the remnants of her tears, Allison stood and crossed to the door.

She must have looked a disaster, since Taffy looked taken aback and demanded, "Are you all right?"

"Yes, I'm fine. Or I will be. What is it you want?"

"Maybe this isn't the right time," Taffy said, hesitation her voice.

Allison fumed. She never liked being coddled, even when she deserved it. This time she'd brought this on herself. "If it's important enough to bring you here, Taffy, then it's important enough for me to hear now."

"If you're sure," Taffy sucked in a deep breath as if to prepare herself. "I did some research on the Web and found this." She handed Allison a sheaf of papers. "It turns out our friend Jay has quite a past with women. He's not just up here to help solve a case, but to wait out the fallout over an affair he had with a district attorney's wife. According to her, he instigated the affair, then dropped her after he'd gotten what he wanted—when she'd put in a good word with his boss for a promotion. He and his department denied that, of course."

Allison scanned the articles, one written just over a week ago, while Paige peeked over her shoulder. They verified what Taffy had said: that Jay had been accused of using a married woman to further his career. In one article, he even admitted to the affair, but claimed he had no knowledge of her marriage. But was he telling the truth?

Maybe he'd known all along who Allison had been, and had hoped being involved with a famous author would help his career, until he thought that she'd been with him for less than honest reasons

Pain, mingling with humiliation and a soul numbing sadness, tore at Allison. His hypocrisy added another dimension to her loss. Her lips trembled at the thought that last night had been a lie. She'd been sucked in by her belief in his sincerity and by the strength of his passion. If not for his strange reaction to the book cover, she'd still be living that lie.

"I know you probably won't believe me, Allison, but I really hated to tell you this," Taffy said. "Jay actually did me a favor when he treated me that way at your party. I did some heavy thinking after that; I'm not happy with myself and I'm going to do some changing. I just wish Jay had been what he'd seemed to be."

Taffy seemed very sincere, but Allison didn't trust her own ability to judge people correctly anymore. She decided, however, to give her the benefit of the doubt.

"I hope you succeed, Taffy. And thank you for telling me, although it doesn't matter. I found out what he's like for myself." She could see the curiosity on the other woman's face, but Allison didn't feel like rehashing it again. She needed to think of a polite way to say goodbye and shut the door.

Before she could do so, her phone rang. Paige answered it, then quickly handed it to Allison. It was her editor.

"Allison, this is Carmela. I'm sorry it took me so long to get back to you, but I think I found the information you wanted. I have the release form signed by the model for your book cover. His name is Jay Cantrall."

Allison's mouth tightened as her heart shattered again, then chilled in an icy bubble. So he'd lied to her when he'd said it wasn't him. Now she had proof, but his bizarre behavior truly didn't make any sense.

"Could you fax that to me please, Carmela? And thank you so much for finding that out."

"No problem. I'll have my secretary do that right away."

Hanging up the phone, Allison turned to Taffy. "Thanks for the information."

"You're welcome. I hope you feel better."

Taffy walked away, looking back at Allison with open curiosity. To her credit, however, she didn't ask any questions as she left.

Allison shut the door just as Paige commented, "You know she just wants him for herself. It's the only reason she came to tell you."

"You're a cynic."

"And you're too trusting." Paige folded her arms, challenge in her gaze.

Allison's eyes teared up again. "Not any more."

🐱 🐱 🐱

The sun filtered through the bedroom window, rousing Jay from a deep sleep, or it could have been a rather loud thumping as someone pounded on his door. Glancing at the clock, he realized it was past ten in the morning. Today, he returned to L.A.; then he could put this sad episode behind him.

"Jay!" A hysterical, high-pitched voice reached him; loud pounding muffled the words. He knew it wouldn't be Allison. She'd quit trying to contact him days ago. He should have felt relieved, but instead, all he felt was an ugly, dead weight in his chest.

No, it sounded more like Birdie. Something must be wrong. Ignoring the fact he wore only boxer shorts, Jay rolled out of bed. Moving as rapidly as his damaged knee would allow, he pulled the door open.

Birdie stood there, with tears streaming through black streaks of mascara. "Is he here?" She looked past him, frantically searching for someone. Taffy, walking down the hallway, stopped and watched.

"Who?" he asked gruffly, hiding a bit more of his boxers-only clad body behind the door.

"Ping, of course!" Birdie wailed.

"Ping? No. I haven't seen him since yesterday." The dog now made it a habit of visiting Jay to remove any of Birdie's offending outfits. Jay carefully folded them and returned them every evening, running the gauntlet of Birdie's cold stare.

"I got this," she sniffled, handing him a crumpled piece of paper. Her hands shook as he took it. Jay scanned it quickly, then raised his startled eyes to her shattered face.

"This is a—"

"I know what it is!" Birdie screeched, her voice reaching ear-shattering proportions. "It's a ransom note!

"My Ping's been kidnapped!"

Chapter Seventeen

At the sound of Birdie's hysterical cries, Allison and Paige rushed out of her apartment and into the hallway. They found her sobbing into Jay's chest as he attempted to comfort her. Taffy hovered nearby, her face pale.

Paige, who'd been regaling Allison with how sweet and wonderful Pearce had been the night before, shoved her way between Birdie and Taffy. To her credit, Taffy didn't react, but scooted back a few feet, giving the group some space.

Allison ignored Jay's presence; Birdie needed her. She pushed aside the pain the sight of him caused. He didn't matter, she told herself; he wasn't worth her anguish. She owed Birdie so much; how could she let her disastrous one-night fling get in the way of that?

"Birdie, what happened? What's wrong?" Allison put her arm around her friend, alarmed at her breakdown. What could have happened to upset her so? Allison suddenly realized that Ping was nowhere to be seen. "Birdie, where's Ping?"

"He's been kidnapped," Jay told her tersely. "Here." Without removing his hold on Birdie, Jay waved a crumpled piece of paper at Allison. Retrieving it, she began to shake as she scanned the typewritten note. She heard Paige suck in her breath as she read the note over Allison's shoulder.

"Who'd want that ratty dog anyway?" Paige whispered into Allison's ear. Unfortunately, her voice carried to Birdie, who glared at Paige and wailed even louder.

"Paige!" Allison frowned at her friend as she tried to comfort Birdie. "I'm sure he's fine. They don't have any reason to hurt him. We'll get him back in one piece." Glancing back at Paige, Allison added, "Ping is a champion, Paige. You know that. He's worth thousands of dollars in stud fees alone."

Birdie pushed herself away from Jay and looked at him imploringly. "You have to find him for me, Jay! Ping must be so frightened. My poor little baby!"

Jay smiled reassuringly. "I'll try my best. Let me call Pearce and get a couple of plainclothesman here to—"

"No!" Birdie wailed. "The note said no police or they'd hurt him! I only trust you. No other cop. We can't risk Ping that way!"

Allison could hear the frustration in Jay's voice. "Birdie, it's going to take more than me to find him. I don't even know where to start looking. Do you have any idea who might have taken him?"

A loud throat-clearing swiveled everyone toward Taffy. Her face was a vivid picture of shame.

"I think I saw the kidnapper," Taffy said. "I'm sorry, Birdie, I didn't know he had Ping or I would have stopped him. He had a pet carrier and he was getting in his car—"

"Wait a minute," Jay interrupted. "You saw someone with a dog carrier? Can you describe him?"

Taffy nodded. "I got a fairly good look at him. It was only about ten minutes ago, in front of the apartments. He was getting into a little red VW Bug, one of the newer ones. He was young, I'd say twenty at the most. Tall—although not as tall as you, Jay—thin, with sandy brown hair cut fairly short." At her description, Birdie looked startled and her body stiffened under Allison's arm.

Her reaction caught Jay's attention, Allison could tell. "Does that ring a bell?" Jay asked.

To Allison's shock, Birdie nodded her head. "I think... Well, I'm not sure, but it could've been him—"

Allison could see Jay school his features to show patience. "Who might have been him?"

Snuffling loudly, Birdie said, "My nephew, Jacob. He showed up here the other day asking for a loan. I've given him money before, and he just wasted it. I didn't see why I should throw away any more money on him."

Allison stared at her friend. She'd known Birdie for years, but had never heard her mention a nephew, let alone one who had money problems. She knew Birdie had a couple of sisters, although she'd never met them. She'd just assumed they lived a distance away.

"Do you have any idea where we might find him?" Jay became all business, his professionalism enveloping him like a cloak. Allison envied him that; just standing near him tore at her.

"I think I have his address in my apartment. I'll go get it for you."

"Birdie, I'm not sure I can drive with my damaged knee. Let me at least call Pearce."

"No! He'll insist on reporting it. I'll go with you." Birdie sobbed out the words, and her hands shook.

"You're too upset. You won't be much help in your condition," Paige said. "I'll go."

"No, you can't." Birdie wiped away another tear. "Ping doesn't like you. You'll only upset him more, and he's so delicate."

"I'll go."

All heads swiveled towards Allison. She took in the slight shake of Paige's head and the doubt clouding Birdie's face. "If you loan me your car, Birdie."

The older woman gazed at her; Allison grimly forced herself not to look away. Finally, Birdie nodded and headed back to her apartment. Taffy went with her, shocking Allison when she put a comforting arm around Birdie's shoulders. Perhaps the woman truly meant to change.

A tense silence enveloped the others.

Allison didn't want to spend time with Jay. That conniving, two-faced liar didn't rate well with her, but if she could help Birdie by going with him, then she would. Besides, she liked Ping, and didn't want to see anything happen to him.

"If you don't want me to—"

"You don't have to—"

Both Allison and Jay spoke together; Paige waved a hand to cut them off.

"You both need to put aside your differences to help Birdie. I've never seen her like this. If she doesn't get that dog back, she's going to have a nervous breakdown."

Allison clamped down her emotions. Paige was right; Birdie needed her, and if it made her feel better to have Allison with Jay to hunt for Ping, then she would do just that.

"I can probably drive, Allison. The knee's better. I only said that to get Birdie to let me call Pearce. If there's a dog carrier, I'm sure I can handle this. If you have a problem—"

"I don't have a problem." She glared at Jay, knowing her anger blazed in her eyes. "I'll be ready to leave in a few minutes." Twisting on her heel, she headed back into her apartment, slamming the door with a bit more force than she needed.

Okay, that would be the last time she'd let Jay Cantrall get to her. If he could be professional, so could she. And she'd prove it.

🐕 🐕 🐕

Allison's departure left Paige and Jay alone. He could tell by the anger radiating from her that she planned on tearing into him. Well, he wouldn't stand here and take it. But before he could turn and walk away, she reached out and grabbed his arm.

Her touch riled him. Giving her a haughty look filled with disdain that would cow most people, he turned toward her. His demeanor did nothing to slow her down. Words spewed from her like hot coals.

"She's still very upset by your hideous behavior. If you do anything to hurt her even a tiny bit, I'll make your life miserable"

"I don't plan to upset Allison or do anything else with her. As far as I'm concerned, she no longer exists." Jerking away from her, he walked as swiftly as his injured knee would allow back into his apartment.

He felt responsible for Ping's disappearance; if he hadn't started undressing him, the dog wouldn't have abandoned his notoriously infamous bad mood and let anyone touch him. But his new, sunny disposition shone through when he wasn't forced to dress like a canine gigolo. That made him much more approachable, even for a dognapper.

So Jay would do his best to rectify the situation, then he'd head back home. To L.A., where he belonged.

🐕 🐕 🐕

Allison focused all her attention on the task at hand: getting ready to go find Ping. The fact that Jay Cantrall, slime trail extraordinaire, would be in the car next to her was something she'd simply ignore. He didn't matter. He couldn't affect her anymore.

And if she kept chanting that, perhaps she'd start believing it.

She scrubbed her face, then added light blush and lipstick. Since she didn't care if she impressed anyone with her looks, she wet her hair down with a comb and secured it to the base of her neck with a clip. Slipping a pair of sandals on her feet, she was ready to go.

Returning to the hallway, she found Jay, Paige and Birdie waiting for her. Birdie handed her the car keys and a small slip of paper with an address on the south side of town on it.

"Allison, darling, I don't know how I'll ever make this up to you. I know spending time with Jay's going to be hard on you, but there's no one else I trust as much as you with Ping."

Allison hugged her, her heart welling for her friend. Ping's importance to Birdie had never gone unnoticed by Allison. Having never had children, Birdie poured all her love into that little dog. It would be tragic if she lost him now.

"We'll do our best," she told Birdie, smiling bravely.

Birdie stroked her cheek. "I know you will. Oh!" she added, as if a thought had just hit her. "I need your car keys, so I can go to the bank and get the ransom—just in case."

"Birdie," Jay cautioned her, "If they call to set something up, don't go to drop off the ransom without us. Not only would it be foolish, because they could get away and still not give you Ping, but it could be very dangerous."

"Oh, don't worry! I won't do a thing without you. I just want to be ready." She smiled bravely, but Allison could see the tears hovering in her eyes.

"I'll go get the keys and come right back," Allison said, needing to get away from Jay. Just a whiff of his aftershave and she felt her knees turning to mush.

She found her keys on her computer desk. Picking them up, she turned to go, then saw the fax lying beside them. Setting down both sets of keys and the address, she picked it up and reread it.

She seethed in annoyance once again as her eyes found what she was looking for: the model's signature. The bold signature read 'J. Cantrall.'

She folded it up and placed it in her pocket, grabbed the keys and trounced out to the hallway. Maybe she'd ask Mr. 'J' Cantrall for an explanation later.

Birdie and Ping were her main concerns right now.

🐾 🐾 🐾

They were a few blocks from the apartments when Jay asked, "May I see the address, please?"

Allison started digging in her pocket and realization dawned on her. She'd left the paper Birdie had given her sitting on her computer desk!

With a murmur of impatience, she braked, then turned the car around in a parking lot. She ignored Jay's sly grin. She didn't need him telling her that she'd messed up. His following chuckle, however, erupted a rush of anger that couldn't be tamped down.

"Listen, you lying hypocrite! I'm only here to help out Birdie and get Ping back. I'm not here for your amusement, so if you could sit there and be quiet—"

Jay barked. "Lying? How do you get off calling me that?"

She didn't need to glance at him to know his eyes bored into her. "I have proof in my pocket that you're a liar, so I feel rather free calling you that."

Jay snorted. "I'd love to see the so-called proof. I've never lied to you, Allie, so I'd like to know how you could have anything proving otherwise."

"Don't call me that," she gritted out. His endearment reminded her of their night together, how close she'd felt to him, how completed she'd been by him. "If you want to see my proof, hold on and I'll show you."

She pulled in another parking lot, unbuckled her seat belt and reached into her pocket. She found the crumpled paper, removed it and handed to him. She studied his face as he unfolded and read it.

His face gave nothing away; his eyes lifted to meet hers. "This is it? A contract with a signature on it, and you're calling me a liar?" Refolding it, he tossed it on her lap.

She couldn't believe his reaction. "That's the contract for the book cover of you that you reacted so strongly to."

"I realize that. I'm just not sure why you're showing me."

"Why?" Allison gasped her disbelief. "You told me that wasn't you!"

"And it's not." Jay's grin twisted grimly. "Is this act trying to prove something?"

His contempt tore at her. "What does that mean?"

"You're not very good at this lying thing, are you, Allie? If you were smart enough to get me up here for your little fantasy, then you had to know my connection to my brother, who, by the way, signs all his contracts with his first initial."

"Your brother? You're telling me that you have a brother who looks just like you, who posed for my book?"

Jay's face tightened. "Now that was better. If I hadn't known any better, I might have believed you."

Allison's voice shook with anger. "I had nothing to do with your being in Spokane. I don't know anything about your brother or how he signs his contracts. You used me; you have a history of using women for your own purposes, and I'm not dumb enough to worry anymore about what you think." Slamming her seat belt on, Allison shifted the car into gear. "Let's just get this over with."

Jay's hand covered hers, stopping her in mid-gear. "No, I'd rather straighten this out now. Did you or did you not coerce my captain into transferring me up here so you could play out this little game of yours?"

"I don't even know your captain, nor do I want to ever know another cop again. So that's your excuse for your bizarre behavior the other morning? You can't admit that your affair with someone's wife got you sent up here? Somehow it has to be my fault?" She laughed with disbelief. "Boy, you really had to dig deep to run away from me, didn't you? What was the excuse you used on the woman in L.A.? Hopefully you didn't drag out this 'brother' one on her.

"Now, if you don't mind," she continued, her throat raw from emotion. "Kindly shut up until this is all over with."

"Gladly." He jerked his hand away from her arm. His one word told her everything: whatever had blossomed between them before could now be considered dead.

She fought back tears as she tried to focus on the road. Her skin burned from where his palm had rested.

Pulling the car into traffic, she concentrated on driving. She battled to control her jangled emotions and the raw ache that her world seemed to rotate around. Her determination got her as far as back to the apartment complex; she didn't know if she'd be able to continue.

Pulling into the parking lot, Jay's hand grabbed her arm. "Stop," he ordered.

Unthinkingly, she slammed on the brakes. "What is it?"

Pointing out the window, Jay motioned toward a figure crossing the lot before them, unaware that they were watching her. "What's she up to? That bag she's carrying looks awfully heavy for a trip to the bank."

Allison followed his gaze, landing on Birdie carrying a large, floral duffel bag. From its bulging middle, she could tell it was stuffed full. She didn't seem to be frightened; Birdie strode with purpose, honing in on Allison's car. Even her face seemed different, full of determination instead of the blank pleasantness that usually cloaked her.

No, Birdie definitely was up to something. Allison needed to find out what.

Chapter Eighteen

"What's she doing *now?*" Allison's question came out as a wail, but Jay didn't blame her. For the last half hour, they'd followed the older woman on a bizarre field trip that had led to a post office, vet's office, dry cleaner and now a gas station, where she'd promptly disappeared inside, dragging the dry cleaning bags and the heavy duffel sack with her. They'd been waiting for her to reappear for several minutes now, and the uneasy feeling in the pit of Jay's stomach grew.

"Just be patient. We can see both exits from here. She can't leave without us seeing her." Allison had parked Birdie's car behind a U-Haul truck next door to the gas station; both of them stood hidden behind the truck, peering out around it toward the station convenience store entrances.

A woman exited the store; it took Jay several moments to realize it was Birdie transformed. And the transformation…! If she hadn't been carrying the same duffel bag, he'd have overlooked her. Her hair, usually overly teased, now lay softly about her face. Her heavy makeup had been replaced with softer hues that lent an air of sophistication to her. Instead of her usual loud clothing, she wore a flowing gold and umber blouse with a matching skirt that flattered her large figure. A pair of sensible pumps, without the normal feathers attached, adorned her feet.

Even as Jay marveled at the changes, he wondered—which Birdie represented the real woman?

At Allison's gasp beside him, he knew she finally recognized her friend. He pulled her back from the trailer and gestured toward the car. "Come on. We don't want to lose her now."

Allison automatically headed for the driver's seat as Jay hesitated. She'd done a wonderful job tailing Birdie so far; with little direction from him, she'd stayed back, even using other vehicles to hide behind. He'd been impressed by her skills, which she'd confessed were picked up from reading detective novels and not from any practical experience.

No, he didn't pause because of her driving. He honestly didn't know if he could stand to be enclosed with her again and not touch her. Her scent of light shampoo and elusive fruity essence reminded him of waking up with her in his arms. Her shoulders, left bare by the plain gray tank top she wore, beckoned for him to caress the silky skin and feel the heat generated by the contact.

Allison, apparently realizing he hadn't moved, turned back toward him, her brows arching up into her cinnamon curls. He remembered one of them tickling his nose as he'd held her, and he'd brushed it aside. Right now he wanted to smooth it away from her brow, kiss the exposed skin, and tell her it would be all right. The concern blazing in her impossibly blue eyes tore at him. He could barely remember why he'd been so upset with her.

Because she used you. Because she's really interested in Ben Stark, not you. Why can't you focus on that?

Because none of that gelled with the innocence radiating from her, or the sincere passion she'd shared with him as they'd made love. Because his heart cried out for her.

He slid into the passenger's seat, and Allison started the car, pulling it forward to give them a view of Birdie as she stowed the duffel bag in the tiny trunk of Allison's car.

A few minutes later, she'd led them to the local mall, outside a trendy burger joint situated in the parking lot. Birdie disappeared inside; Jay swiftly flew into action.

"Drive around the back," he said. Allison followed the same pattern she'd done since their adventure had started; without question, she followed his instructions. Jay wished most of his former partners had been so amenable. Her acquiescence worried him a bit, though. She'd been strangely still and pale, void of her normal feistiness.

Allison pulled behind the restaurant and killed the engine. "What now?" she whispered. Jay almost laughed at her soft voice; they didn't need to whisper in the car, but one look at her tight lips and he knew his humor might be her breaking point. He could only imagine how she felt watching her trusted friend lay down such an elaborate trail just to go to lunch. Something about Birdie Talbot didn't pan out.

Allison's fragility called to him; reaching across, he gripped her fingers. Their iciness in the summer heat shocked him; his thumb rubbed across them in an attempt to transfer some warmth.

"We go in and see who she's meeting, see if we can get close enough to find out what's going on without her seeing us." He didn't ask her if she wanted to stay in the car; he knew her enough to understand she needed to see for herself.

They reached the back door just as a young teen in a white uniform emerged. Jay dropped Allison's hand and produced his badge.

"Spokane PD on an investigation," he said. "Could you get your manager for us? And please keep this low-keyed," he added as the boy's eyes bulged and his Adam's apple bobbed.

"Sure, I'll be right back!" he said, disappearing into the kitchen. Jay followed, pulling Allison in behind him.

He crossed over to the door that separated the kitchen from the restaurant. Peering through the long, narrow window, he saw a smiling hostess leading Birdie toward a booth.

The uniformed teen they'd talked to earlier returned, followed by a confused-looking man in a dark suit. Jay stood back from the door as they pushed through.

Introductions commenced, then Jay stated his intent. "We're working on a kidnapping case. A woman entering this place is the key to cracking it. We need to observe her, see who she's meeting, without her being aware of us."

The manager nodded in understanding, although his confusion remained apparent in his eyes. "Of course. If you could describe her, we'll get you an adjoining booth. The partitions are high enough that she won't see you, although I'm not certain how much you'll be able to hear."

"Your hostess just walked by with her. She's wearing..."

As Jay described Birdie in her new persona, he became aware of Allison pressing against the back of his shoulder, straining to listen over the rattle of dishes and the kitchen staff's loud clamor. Her fingers gripped his arm, as if she needed him to lean on. The thought that this tough woman needed him to bolster her moved something deep inside him.

His former suspicions began to melt away; maybe there was some other explanation for all these bizarre coincidences. He'd seen nothing in her make-up that would allow her to be so deceitful. His instincts told him she couldn't go against her basic nature. Slipping his hand back toward her, he found her chilled fingers and squeezed them briefly.

She clung to him, not letting him go.

"Do you mean Mrs. Tyler?" the manager asked. "She comes here every couple of weeks to have lunch with her two nephews. I can't imagine what trouble she could be in."

Jay frowned. *Tyler?* "The woman your hostess just seated, her name is Birdie Talbot." *Why would Birdie be using a different name?*

The uniformed teenager offered, "I'll go check with Natalie," and rushed out the door, nearly smacking into a waiter heading into the kitchen. The remaining trio moved out of his way, clustering closely together to let the man through. Jay felt Allison's breasts crushed up against his back; he tamped down on the rush of heat that hit him full force. His breath eased when she finally moved away from him, although her death-grip on his hand never ceased.

In a few moments, the teen returned. "That's got to be her," he told them. "Only person even close to your suspect, and Natalie says she's the only one that's arrived in the last few minutes." His eager face lit with excitement.

Allison stiffened beside Jay; how she felt about this strange set of circumstances he couldn't imagine.

"Right," Jay said. "Then could you set us up a booth? One where anyone joining her wouldn't walk by." He doubted anyone would recognize him, but he couldn't be sure about Allison. No reason to take chances.

They settled themselves against the divider in the adjoining booth nearest Birdie, menus in hand. The same young waiter busily arranged their silverware and water, then began to hover.

Finally, Jay hissed at him, "You're going to ruin this. Get out of here." He hated the hurt look that emerged on the guy's face. To soften it, he pulled a business card out of his wallet, wrote down his cell number and handed it to him. "Call me tomorrow and I'll fill you in on what I can, okay?"

Happily the boy snatched the card and rushed off past Birdie's booth. Sitting nearest the aisle, Jay followed his progress, hoping he'd keep moving. On his way, the waiter passed a young man in his late teens or early twenties, wearing khakis and a white shirt, whose eyes lit on Birdie. His face broke into a huge grin.

"Aunt Robbie! You look beautiful as always!"

Birdie slid out of the booth to embrace the young man. Jay whipped his head back around so she couldn't see him. *Aunt Robbie?*

"Darling! And you're handsome as always." Jay could hear a rustle; they must have hugged.

Jay whispered to Allison, "Do you know her nephew?"

She shook her head. "No. She's mentioned sisters, but never nephews. I didn't know until she gave us that address that any existed, or that she met with them so frequently."

Jay's frown deepened. This made no sense. Why keep them secret from Allison? He could understand if she might be ashamed of the one who apparently borrowed money all the time, but to hide family get-togethers? Nothing here was clear.

"Here's your copy of my latest," Birdie said. "It's due to hit the stands in about a month. So, how's your brother Jacob doing in Alaska?"

Allison's breath froze in her throat as she listened to Birdie—Robbie—ask about the well-being of a nephew who only an hour ago, she'd accused of stealing Ping. And what was this about something hitting the stands? Sounded like she was talking about a book.

She didn't understand any of this.

The young man laughed. "I called him this morning. He loves it and hates it. Says Juneau is the deadest town, and then told me about chasing a moose with his truck off a main highway." The man paused, then added, "He said to tell you he'll be down for a visit sometime next month, then home for good by October. And he thanked you again for letting him keep his apartment rent-free while he was gone."

Allison's throat went dry as the implications hit her. They'd been sent on a wild-goose chase; no way could Jacob have taken Ping! And the apartment he spoke of must be in one of the other apartment houses Birdie owned. But why would Birdie do something like this?

"No problem, darling. It's not like I need the money." Allison heard a light thunk as a glass settled down on their table. She picked up her own and took a sip. "So did Ping give you any trouble when you dropped him off this morning? And did you see his girlfriend? I stopped by on my way here; she's going to have incredibly beautiful puppies."

Puppies? Ping wasn't kidnapped? Birdie had sent him off to a breeding session? Allison sucked water in the wrong way and began to choke. Water sloshed on her hand as she set her glass down loudly and hacked for air.

"No, she hadn't arrived when I dropped him off. He behaved fairly well for me, although I don't understand why you asked me to take him there instead of dropping him off yourself."

Jay whacked her on the back and Allison glared at him angrily as she continued to hack.

"Because I'm trying to help Allison with her new relationship. I think she's in love... Aaron, that woman in the adjoining booth is choking!"

Allison's eyes widened in horror as she tried to breathe; Jay whacked her again just as she reached for her water glass to try taking another sip. Her hand collided with the glass, sending it skidding into the aisle. Water cascaded down the front of her and onto Jay.

Her involuntary gasp of shock as the icy water hit her increased the coughing fit; her eyes watered as Jay smacked her once more. She grabbed his water and barely got a sip down before Birdie and her nephew rounded the corner.

She sucked in a shallow breath as she watched Birdie's face with trepidation and a bit of defiance. Then her eyes traveled to the nephew. The pain of unexpected recognition hit her like a wave; she forgot to breathe as she stared at him. She gripped Jay's arm as one would a lifeline—only his warmth kept her tethered in this bizarre world she'd suddenly entered.

Aaron, Birdie had called him. Aaron Tensley. He was older, but still had the same face that had stared at her in terror over seven years before; the face clinging to that rock face. That face that had changed her entire life.

He was Birdie's nephew.

Chapter Nineteen

"Oh, Allison." Birdie stared at her in disappointment. "You followed me."

Disbelief sizzled in Allison as she coughed, swallowed some more of Jay's water, then choked out her words. "You can't be upset with *me!* I'm not the one who's been playing this…this grand deception for years!" She wheezed, took another sip, ignored her watery eyes. "Care to explain why you did this? And what's your real name, *Birdie?* Is it Birdie Talbot or Robbie Tyler?"

Robbie Tyler—the name struck her as it ran through her head. Robbie Tyler. A book to be released soon. A chill filled her; it couldn't be!

"You—" She began to cough again. Taking another sip of Jay's water, she rasped, "You're Robert Tyler, aren't you?"

Birdie and Aaron shared glances. "I never thought it would go this far, Allison. I'm sorry," Aaron told her. "I wanted to fix things for you after the accident. I know what my mom had said to you, threatening you if you tried to contact me. I know you blamed yourself for the accident, but it wasn't your fault. My mom wouldn't let me get in touch with you, so I asked Aunt Robbie to help me."

Jay looked from Allison to Aaron, his confusion apparent. "I thought you said you've never met Birdie's nephews."

"I didn't know I had," she replied. She could breathe normally now; her voice became less hoarse with each word. "I've met this one, though. Jay, meet Aaron Tensley. This is the boy I told you about, the one who fell from the cliff." Her voice broke; taking a sip of water, she continued. "Aaron, this is Jay Cantrall. Your Aunt 'Robbie' asked him to help find Ping, who, she told us in a rather convincing manner, had been kidnapped by your brother, Jacob."

"Aunt Robbie, you didn't! Why would you do that?"

"Because I wanted Jay and Allison to talk; they've been avoiding each other for days. They're both miserable, neither would listen to reason, and they need to straighten things out before he leaves today. I'd planned on sending them on a long wild-goose chase filled with clues, that would have taken them all day, but when one of the tenants saw you taking Ping, I had to improvise."

"You didn't answer my question," Ice-cold rage filled Allison. She could see a string of manipulation littering her world; how much of her life had been an illusion? "Are you or are you not Robert Tyler?"

Shrugging, Birdie sighed. "Yes, guilty as charged."

Tears stung Allison. "So I was...what? A little project? Were you trying to *get even with me* for Aaron being hurt?"

Eyes widening in shock, Birdie chirped a denial. "No, of course not. You didn't injure Aaron; he knows that his own recklessness caused the accident—and you should know that, too. But you were seriously hurt trying to save him, and Aaron needed some sort of way to help you so the guilt wouldn't tear him apart. He knew that you'd twisted at the last moment and took the brunt of the fall. If you hadn't, he probably would have died. He asked me to help you get your life back. That's all I've wanted. If I'd come to you and told you exactly who I was, would you have let me help?"

Allison stared at her as she pondered her question. The answer? No, she wouldn't have. She'd been so burdened with guilt, she wouldn't have been able to let anyone around her.

Birdie read her silence clearly. "No, I didn't think so. Darling, I took one look at you in that hospital bed, and saw how much it cost you to save my nephew, and I loved you right then. Then I found out you were alone, that your family barely even showed up at the hospital… Well, I couldn't get that picture out of my mind. When you were transferred to the rehab center, I couldn't just sit back and let you be all alone."

Her eyes glittered with tears as she spoke. "I needed to help you, and you needed me. And Aaron needed to help you as well. He felt so guilty causing you to hurt yourself. So I came up with this plan."

Conflicting emotions, anger and gratitude, swirled inside Allison. Then one of Birdie's statements grabbed her attention.

"You said you saw me in the hospital, but I don't remember seeing you there. When was that?"

"Can we sit down?" Birdie asked. At Allison's nod, she and Aaron slid onto the bench opposite Allison and Jay. Once they were situated, Birdie continued.

"I came to the hospital the night of the accident. Aaron was scared and upset that his behavior had caused you to get hurt, so I sat with him while my sister went to get something to eat, or so she told me. When she didn't come back right away, I went looking for her, and found her down the hallway shouting at you. The nurses were trying to pull her out of your room and she kept screaming that it was your fault. I grabbed her and yelled at her to stop, then dragged her out of there. You stared at me the entire time, tears running down your face." Birdie sighed. "That's one reason I changed my appearance when I came to see you at the rehab center. I thought you might recognize me."

"I don't remember you," Allison whispered. "I remember her screaming at me. Those words are burnt in my mind."

It's your fault he's lying there! It's your fault he almost died! Do you realize that you've destroyed his future, that he might never walk again?

Yes, she'd never forgotten those accusations, hurled at her with the brute force of a mother's pain. Hot tears burned her eyes; she felt Jay's strong presence next to her. Sucking in a deep breath, she reached for his hand under the cover of the table. His fingers engulfed hers, the warmth anchored her.

Aaron smiled at her. "I knew I'd get better. But I worried about you. When I thought about how my mom treated you, even after I told her you were only trying to help me, it really bothered me. So Aunt Robbie said she'd help you. I'm sorry if it seems we deceived you."

His serious eyes swam with the pain he must have felt. Had time not dulled the memories for him? Allison still remembered that day, but she'd tempered the ache with her efforts to create a place that would help people with the same types of injuries she'd sustained. Had Allison become Aaron's project in the same way, to help him through the pain?

"So what's your real name?" she asked Birdie.

"Tyler is my maiden name," she replied. "Talbot is my married. I go by Birdie or Robbie. My family calls me Robbie; everyone else calls me Birdie. So you know me by my 'real' name."

"And the scatter-brained act? How much of that's real and how much was for Allison's benefit?" Jay asked.

Birdie laughed. "My family would say that all of it's real, but I have to admit that people are a little more forgiving when they think you're a bit soft in the head. I can get away with more being Birdie Talbot than poor Robbie Tyler ever will."

Allison felt Jay's shoulder press against her. A tiny thrill bubbled through her. She wished she could depend on that closeness, that feeling of oneness she'd shared with him. But like many things in her life, she'd found him to be an illusion. Perhaps even one she'd woven herself.

Just like her friendship with Birdie had turned out to be an illusion. How much of her life was based on lies?

"The apartment," Suspicion struck her. "Jay's apartment. Why do you keep evicting everyone from that unit?"

Birdie blushed, but didn't reply. Aaron eyed her, then shook his head. "I'm afraid that part isn't an act. My Aunt Robbie suffers from a serious case of match-making fever. She's done it forever. She fixed up my parents, my cousins, my aunts and uncles, grocery clerks she likes, even the mailman at her other apartment complex. She doesn't just stop at introductions, either. She's set up 'accidental' meetings, arranged little scenes, like Ping's 'kidnapping' today. I sometimes help her with the accounting books—business is my major—and I saw what she was doing with that unit quite a while ago. So, yeah, she was trying to find you someone."

Suddenly Allison couldn't hear any more. Illusions, games, deceptions—it was too much. She shoved on Jay, who was blocking her way. "I need to go."

"Allison—" Birdie protested.

Allison shook her head. "I can't talk to you now. Not yet. I'll say something that someday I might regret." Jay slid out of the booth, and Allison bolted, nearly stepping on her discarded water glass. She stopped, turned to Aaron. "I'm glad you're okay. I always wondered…"

He smiled. "I'm glad you're okay, too. And I want you to know—my mom doesn't blame you any more. That was just her knee-jerk reaction."

Allison would have smiled at that gift if she wasn't so shell-shocked. "Thanks." Then she turned and fled everything. Birdie, all her lies—what else had she arranged? Jay's very presence in Spokane?—Jay, everything.

But unfortunately everything didn't stay where it should. As she burst from the restaurant, then stopped and placed hands on knees to suck in some deep breaths, she felt a hand on her back and knew that touch instantly. Jay. Would her body ever forget?

More important, would her heart?

"Are you all right?" he asked. She nodded, then straightened up, pulling away from him. Pushing her hair from her face, she walked over to Birdie's car, Jay following behind her. Pushing the remote button, she climbed in, then forced herself to hook the seat belt. She was acutely aware of Jay doing the same beside her.

Jamming the key in the ignition, she watched her hands shake. Reaction hit her, hard. Her head bobbed forward, settling on the steering wheel. Closing her eyes, she sucked in deep breaths, hoping that somehow she could pull herself together, find the strength to drive home.

"Allie," Jay's hand curved around her left shoulder. "You're in shock. Take a few minutes. We're in no hurry."

His flight. Realization crashed into her. She'd been avoiding this, hiding in her apartment, writing like a fiend. Jay would be leaving today, and she'd never see him again.

After the way he'd treated her, it shouldn't matter. In fact, it should be a relief to have him gone. Instead, it mattered too much, and her heart screamed at the thought of him disappearing, even though her head wanted to shout, *Good riddance!*

His right hand smoothed her hair from her cheek, tucking it behind her ear. She wanted to shake it loose, hide behind the veil of curls. "Don't you have a plane to catch?"

"It's not until later today. Birdie timed this well. I wondered why she asked me about flight times the other day. Now I know." His thumb caressed her shoulder, seemingly without thought as he continued talking. "Who would have guessed that scatterbrained woman could hide such a clever nature?"

"Clever?" Allison snorted. "Try devious. Twisted. Try—"

"Allison," Jay's soft voice chided her. "She did it because she cares for you, and because she loves her nephew. Keep that in mind before you judge her too harshly."

His gentle acceptance of Birdie's actions shocked her. Twisting her head, she opened her eyes to find his somber gaze fixed on her face. "How can you say that? She manipulated you, too. She planted you next door to me so that we could meet and see if we were 'compatible.' Heck, why stop there? Maybe she even arranged for your transfer, like you accused me of doing."

"Then she did me a favor," Stunned, Allison lifted her head to stare at him. "I needed this, getting away from L.A. and letting everything down there roll over. You mentioned the affair earlier, the one I supposedly had." She nodded, and he grimaced. "Yeah, there's a mess. She recanted her story, by the way, under pressure of the Department. She admitted that I didn't know who she was, therefore I had no ulterior motives to becoming involved with her. I'll have to remember to do a background check on anyone I get involved with, to avoid garbage like that."

Allison winced, feeling those words aimed at her. Jay shook his denial. "I didn't mean you. Looking back, and considering what I learned about Birdie today, I realize that even if you hid your true identity from me, that's your business. I wasn't exactly forthcoming with my past, either. Guess we were a little preoccupied to share little details, like the fact you're a famous author and I have a brother who's a fairly successful actor."

His mouth quirked into a semblance of a smile, and Allison's spirits lifted slightly. "Yeah, preoccupations like rescuing you from pint-sized attackers."

Jay laughed. "I would have preferred protection before the attacks."

Allison grinned, leaning back into the seat, feeling his arm still wrapped around her. It felt too good to ask him to remove it.

"I'm sorry."

His apology caught her by surprise. "For what?"

He shrugged. "For jumping to conclusions. For accusing you of trying to manipulate me. For lumping you in the same category as…" He grimaced. "I knew from the moment I met you that you're incapable of stuff like that. I let facts cloud my instincts."

She studied his eyes for a moment, finding sincerity in their depths. And something else, something that warmed her blood. "Apology accepted. And I'm sorry I thought you a fortune-hunting creep."

Jay laughed, the sound rippling through Allison. "Honestly, Allie, if I was an opportunist, I'd look for someone whose lifestyle was a bit more lavish. Not that I'm not impressed with the Hot Wheels collection, but several real wheels would be more impressive," His smile faded as he studied her. "You invest all your money into that clinic, don't you? You don't just work there. It's your pet project, isn't it?"

She nodded, and he stroked her cheek. "Allie, here you are, trying to make up for what happened to that boy, and he's doing the same for you."

She resisted leaning into his hand. "Yeah, I guess we are. Strange," She shuddered. "The whole thing is so bizarre." She pulled away, distrusting the intimate air surrounding them. He'd still be leaving. Nothing had changed.

She started the car, effectively distancing herself from him. With a sigh, he removed his arm from around her, leaned back into his seat and stared out the window.

"I need to go home, Allie," he said. "L.A. is where I grew up. I've made a decent life for myself there. I put in for a promotion, passed all the exams. Next opening, I'm there."

She reversed out of the parking slot, put the car into forward and pulled out of the lot. All the time, pain pushed tears into burning the back of her eyes. "I know."

"I can't ask you to move down there. That's not fair to you. And face it, what do we really have in common? You're a famous author, I'm a cop. You're into doing nice things for people. I'm too jaded to see the point."

"You did something nice for Paige and Pearce." She was amazed at how normal her voice sounded as she stopped for a red light. Turning on her blinker, she made a right turn.

"Because it fit my plans at the time."

"I see." But she didn't. She'd watched him with Ping, witnessed his tenderness with Birdie during her 'Ping kidnapping' act. That didn't come from a hardened heart, but from someone who cared. Didn't he realize that?

She drove in silence back to the apartment complex, pulling into Birdie's reserved spot. She didn't know what to say, or if she should say anything. He was determined to walk away, and he was right, her life was here. But for him, she'd face L.A.'s congestion, pollution, even earthquakes. If only he'd ask. If only he cared enough to ask.

Turning off the car and removing the keys, she hesitated too long before getting out and heading to her safe, sequestered home.

"Allison," Jay's hand on her forearm held her back. "You do understand, don't you? You have your life. I have mine." His mouth twisted without humor. "After all, it's not like we're in love, is it?"

Fishing. Was he fishing? Did he love her and needed her to say the words first? She searched his face for some sign, for something there that would give her a clue as to why he'd said that. But the old Jay met her gaze, the one whose remoteness had so frustrated her when they'd first met.

She couldn't do it. She couldn't make that leap of faith. Not without something from him first. So she chose the safe path

"No," she whispered softly. "It's not like we're in love."

🐾 🐾 🐾

"Jay," He looked up from his desk in L.A., where'd he'd sat for the last few days, shuffling paperwork around, waiting for the doctor to release him back to field work. His partner, Stan, hovered above him, juggling a coffee cup and a white paper bag. "Got you some lunch. Hope you're hungry."

"Thanks." No use telling him that his appetite had stayed in Spokane. Along with his heart.

He took the coffee and the sack, knowing from the smell, it contained something with onions. He popped the lid off the dark brew. A sip informed him his gut wouldn't welcome coffee, either.

Damn it, he wanted his life back. All the hoopla over the affair had died down the first ten minutes after he'd returned. But he found he couldn't concentrate on anything. All he could see were Allison's dazzling blue eyes.

And the hurt she'd tried to hide from him when he'd left her.

"Jay," Stan's voice hinted at impatience. Startled, he looked back up to find his partner still standing there.

The other man's eyes narrowed at he watched Jay. Jay forced his expression to give nothing away, to remain remote and unreadable, but it was too late. Stan knew him too well.

"Why'd you come back? You've left something there, right? Let me guess. A woman."

He didn't reply. He didn't need to. His partner would know by the tightening of his neck muscles that Allison had rampaged back into his thoughts.

Allison. Paint dripping from her hair as she'd stood, looking at him in shock. Anger shot at him when he'd made disparaging remarks about Ping.

And her eyes glowing in the dark, sated with pleasure as he'd stroked her hair after they'd made love.

And he'd walked away from her.

He hadn't called her since returning. He didn't know if he could hear her voice and still control the longing that threatened to override common sense and toss him on a plane straight to Spokane. So he stared at the phone every night, running through what he'd say to her but never picking up the receiver.

"You're afraid of rejection, man. You're just like I was when I found Melody." Stan and Melody had married the first year Jay and Stan had been partners.

Rejection. Just the word churned Jay's stomach. Could Stan be right?

Jay knew Stan and Melody's history. They'd broken up, stayed apart for six months, until Stan had seen Melody one night—with another man. He'd told Jay the next day his old life was over, and the only way to have a new life was to win her back. And he had.

Jay thought of how he'd feel if he saw Allie with another guy. The acidic burning in his gut told him the answer.

"I talked to the Captain," Stan said, as he sat in the chair opposite Jay. "He looked into it for me. Spokane PD will take you back on a permanent basis. Said you did a good job for them until you decided to take up canine obstacle courses."

Jay's heart thudded to a stop. "Have I been that bad at my job?"

Stan laughed. "No, you've been your usual self. Hard-working. Thorough. But your eyes gave it all away to me. Your heart isn't here anymore, partner. You left it somewhere else. You need to face it, buddy, and own up to the fact that L.A. isn't your home anymore." Stan's gaze sobered. "At least, not until you resolve whatever it is between you and that woman."

Jay stared into his coffee. His pulse pounded in his ears. He'd denied the truth since getting back, but Stan's words brought it home. He didn't want to be here. He felt remote, disconnected from his old life. He kept wondering: had Pearce found a new partner yet? Had he and Paige set a date? And Ping—was the goofy mutt back to being a cranky bastard, or was Birdie cutting him some slack about the outfits?

Then there was Allison. He knew he'd hurt her horribly by leaving her. Could he find a way to convince her to give him another chance?

Poor choices. Rejection or continuing to feel like this. Either way, he could end up alone. There was only one way to end up with Allie.

He'd have to go home.

🐾 🐾 🐾

Her blank stare into nothingness told him everything; Jay didn't need to touch her to know she was gone, torn from him forever.

"Em." *Her name ripped from his chest; deep within him, his world shattered. All that was genuine and good and treasured in his life now lay dead before him, her blood pooled about her—*

"Damn." Sniffling loudly, Allison wiped away her tears with the back of her hand. She'd done it again. She'd typed Jay's name instead of Ben's.

Well, she couldn't help the boo-boos. She knew that Jay was nothing like Ben, but she couldn't concentrate on her detective. No, her mush-for-brains insisted upon obsessing over the man she couldn't have. But she needed to let him go. A week had passed since Jay'd returned to Los Angeles, a week in which he hadn't called. A week where she'd missed him more than she could have imagined possible.

All she'd done since he'd left was work on her book. She buried herself deep in her story and her characters in an attempt to stave off the pain, and now, she'd reached Emily's death scene. As usual, she'd become a crying, sobbing mess. On top of Emily, she nursed a broken heart, which didn't make surviving this particular death scene any easier.

Hiccupping loudly, she ignored the 'Jay' staring back at her from the computer monitor. She'd do a word search later and kill all those nasty Jays that had crept into her writing.

"Em." Touching her rapidly cooling cheek, he savaged himself for letting her down, letting this happen to her. She'd been too precious to ever put in danger, yet time and again, he'd let her leap into the fray. Damn, he'd even admired her for it.

She felt so soft, so smooth, like a priceless silk so rare, a person would be lucky to touch it once in a lifetime. He'd never know what it would be like to tease her again, to share his deepest thoughts with her. How could he survive without his Em?

Allison sobbed. Her fingers stumbled to a halt. She considered taking a break, maybe going for a walk. Or taking Ping for a walk. She and Birdie had a tentative peace; Allison understood why she'd done what she'd done, but the other woman needed to come to grips with the fact that matchmaking was out of the question. Ever.

No, she needed to finish this. She needed to move on with her book. And once it was done, she'd move on with her life as well.

He couldn't leave her there, not in this cold, filthy warehouse. He needed to—

"Allie!"

Loud pounding made her jump. Heart thumping, Allison recognized the voice with no effort. How could she not? It haunted her every waking and sleeping moment; it followed her through her days and deep into her nights.

Jay. He'd come back.

Her legs threatened to buckle as she rushed toward the door, intending to fling it open, to see his beloved face again, to have his arms crush her against him. Then common sense overrode her roller-coaster of emotions.

No. He'd left her. He'd told her he couldn't live here; he made it clear he couldn't choose her over his work, and he'd left. He hadn't even offered her a glimmer of hope, instead saying goodbye in that remote, dead voice of his.

She wasn't about to let him waltz in here and break her heart all over again.

Leaning her head against the door, she gathered all her strength and forced the words out through stiff lips. "Go away."

"Allie, you don't mean that," His voice, soft and chiding, swirled in her stomach.

Oh, yes, she did. "Oh, yes, I do!"

"Okay, if you won't open up and let me plead my case with you, then let me plead Emily's."

"Emily?" she squeaked. Why on earth did he want to discuss her writing?

"I talked with Paige. She told me you're killing Emily off tonight. Allie, you can't kill her. She deserves to live. She deserves to know some happiness. You know how much she loves Ben. Don't you think they've earned a chance to explore their love? Don't you think that now's the time for him to wake up and realize what a prize Emily is, that she's where his future belongs? No matter where she is or what she does, he needs to be with her."

"No," Her voice rasped out through her pain. Was he talking about Ben or himself? Did he see her as Emily? She forced herself to tamp down on her burgeoning hope. His coming back was a good sign, but that didn't mean he loved her. It could be a simple matter of lust. "Ben knows that now, but it's too late. He could never believe in her. He could never trust his feelings. And now she's dead." She stifled a hiccupping sob.

"It's not too late, Allie," Jay's voice softened so she had to strain to hear it through the door. She thought she could hear tenderness in the tone, and perhaps even a touch of love. "He knows now that it wasn't her he didn't trust, but himself. He couldn't believe that she could love him for himself. He kept thinking that there must be an ulterior motive. But now he knows that she'd never play games. He understands that to win her love, he needs to believe in himself.

"Allie, don't give up. You have the power to make everything right." His voice reverberated through the wooden door; she imagined his mouth mere inches from hers. She could easily envision the hard wood dissolving between them, then his lips capturing hers.

"Allie, are you listening? Can you honestly say they don't deserve a chance?"

Could she live with knowing that she'd turned Jay away? Could she survive another lonely night, knowing that she could have had Jay's strong warm arms wrapped about her, instead of facing that empty bed again?

Could she ever forgive herself for never taking that leap?

"No," she whispered. Her fingers traced the spot that would be at the same level as Jay's mouth. "No," she repeated as joy roared to life within her. "I don't think I can."

She would never remember unlocking the door and pulling it open. All that stuck in her mind was an incredible elation that lifted her off her feet and into his arms.

His mouth found hers, and she drowned in the feel of him, warm and solid against her.

"Allie, I love you," Jay growled against her mouth.

Her arms tightened about his neck as her tears of joy spilled onto his face. "I love you, too."

With a shout of delight, Jay spun around with her in his arms, filling the hallway with laughter.

Unseen by either of them, Birdie Talbot watched the display, then wiped her own tears away. Next to her, Ping moved silently, his steps so smooth, the tiny bell about his neck never sounded.

"Oh, Allison, you've finally found your sunshine," Birdie whispered. Then, without a sound, she stepped back into her apartment, leaving the two lovers alone. Ping followed, his bell jingling only once as Birdie carefully shut the door.

"Did you hear that?" Jay asked Allison, finally allowing her feet to touch the floor.

"Oh, yeah," Allison chortled. "Every time true love wins, an angel rings its bell."

Jay laughed. "I don't think that's quite right," he told her. "But it'll do for now."

The End

Stacia Wolf

If someone tried, they'd have trouble pigeon-holing Stacia. But that's good news for this author—she doesn't mind her numerous roles of writer, artist, photographer, mom, grandmother, home remodeler, designer, gardener, business woman. They all bring out different aspects of her, and offer diverse challenges. Each facet of her life is filled to the brim.

This is all the result of one simple truth about Stacia: "I don't sit still well."

She lays the blame fully on the creative monster hidden inside her that demands equal time, craves to create and experiment. "Sometimes that creature screams for attention. I'm stuck in its wake, trying to get all the ideas out in sort of tangible form. Other times, it's very, very silent. Those times, I can honestly say, are very boring to me."

To Stacia, words are a melody, a catharsis, a way to let the creative soul inside her sing out. Every story she writes, every little twist that comes to her mind, is an exciting journey that she loves to share with others. She's not stuck on any one particular genre. She loves comedies and pure romances; she can become lost in a dramatic situation, and the thought of writing a fantasy – without the boundaries of reality—causes her already crazy imagination to soar. Being published is very gratifying for her. "I know now that someone else will go along for the ride. I also know that it's going to be one hell of a journey."

To learn more, visit her website at www.staciawolf.com

If you loved "You'll Be The Death of Me!" by Stacia Wolf, you'll enjoy this excerpt from

Her Passion
© 2006 Denise Belinda McDonald
Available now from Samhain Publishing.

Can a brief affair sustain a woman before her upcoming, loveless marriage?

Joel Burkhart's life is work, work and more work until he finds that one woman he's compared every other woman to since high school, but she's taken.

Colleen Nance feels her life closing in on her with her nuptials nearing. When passion ignites, she loses her head and loses control.

With a ticking clock, can the pair find what they need in each other or are they destined to continue in a passionless life where status-quo is good enough?

Warning: this title contains explicit sex.

The woman at the counter caught his attention and, he suspected, that of every other male in the room. A shiny green dress hugged her full curvy figure. Her rounded hips tapered up to a waist he wouldn't mind getting his hands around. He liked a woman with a body. Not some pencil-thin waif who looked like she never ate. And even from his spot across the room, he saw the flawless ivory-skinned arms and shoulders. Skin that made his mouth water.

Damn, he needed to get hold of himself and find a seat. But he was rooted in his spot while his eyes feasted on her.

A mass of reddish-brown curls sat atop her head. He wondered what she looked like, what color her eyes were. Joel would bet anything that they sparkled not green as her dress but a deep sapphire blue. He didn't know why he was so certain, but he'd have bet anything he was right.

And already a man preyed upon her. But by the sullen look on his face, she'd shot him down flat.

Joel chuckled to himself.

She turned down Darryl Blackwood and his Casanova charisma.

Joel couldn't remember the last time a woman passed on the office playboy's oozing charm.

"Have a seat, Joel." Steve Sullivan motioned to an empty chair across the table. Steve, Frank, and three other men from the Oklahoma City office surrounded the table.

"Where the heck is that waitress?" Frank looked around the room. "They're too busy tonight. Someone will have to go to the bar for our drinks."

"I'll go." Joel practically jumped out of his seat. He took the men's orders and waded through the crowd.

Joel wanted to get a better look at the woman in green. He told himself he was only curious to know if he was right about her eyes. But there was something else, too, something about her that drew him. Joel's eyes trained on the slim line of her neck and the few curls that had escaped the clip. The auburn tresses danced and swayed with her every move. He wondered how soft her hair would feel running through his fingers. His gut tightened with desire.

She swiveled on her seat. He could almost see her. But someone stepped between them and blocked her from view.

Darryl.

Doesn't he ever give up?

Joel could hear Darryl's slick come-ons. "Hey baby, have you had time to think over my proposition?"

"What's to think about?" Her voice was smooth and sexy.

Damn, Darryl's charm had worked. I walked over here for nothing.

"I already told you I wasn't interested." All the honey and whiskey turned icy cold. "Now, please, for the last time, *go away*."

"Ha!" Joel mumbled under his breath. "Darryl doesn't always get what he wants, after all."

A hard frown creased Darryl's face and two red blotches tinted his cheeks. Accustomed to women jumping at the chance for a date with him—or so the rumors around the office proclaimed—Darryl turned slowly and walked away.

"What is it with these guys? They see a woman sitting alone and can't help but use tired old lines." Her voice settled somewhere between honey and the icy shards she used on Darryl as she spoke to the bartender. But Joel found even her normal voice sexy as hell. "He thinks he's too macho for words." She and the bartender laughed.

"Can I help you, sir?"

Joel jolted out of his trance.

"Ah, yeah I need a, ah…" Joel's mind went blank with the drink orders. *Think fast man.* "Two pitchers of beer."

Joel eased onto the stool. He turned his head, trying to get a better glimpse of the woman. All the while he chastised himself for acting like a damn fool. He couldn't remember being that tongue-tied—at least not since high school.

The woman must have felt his gaze because she tilted her head in Joel's direction. As time and motion slowed, his mind flashed to high school with a niggling sense of déjà vu. The last female to put him in such a stupor was…

Colleen Nance.

Colleen's lips quirked up on the side and her eyebrows rose slightly. As Joel stared, his chin all but fell to his chest. He had to force his mouth shut to return the smile.

His mind reeled.

Colleen Nance looked at him, the smile unwavering. And yes, her eyes were blue—not something you found often with the auburn hair rampant in her family. The same dynamic azure he remembered from high school. Her hair was darker though. Even after thirteen years, the power of his youthful lust hadn't lessened one iota.

He expected her to say something, anything. It had been a little over thirteen years since the fateful night of senior prom, thirteen years since either of them had seen one another at graduation.

The smile slid from her face and she turned her attention back to her drink. He watched her shoulders rise and fall with a heavy sigh.

Why isn't she speaking to me?

"How have…"

"Here you go, sir." The bartender sat the pitchers and several plastic cups down.

"Thanks." Joel pulled out two bills and handed them across the counter. He moved his attention back to Colleen but she'd swiveled in her seat again and presented her back to him.

I guess it's been too many years. She must not want to rekindle high school memories.

Disappointed, Joel hefted the pitchers and cups and walked back to the table then set the beer down.

"Hey, man. What happened to our drinks?"

"Huh? What?"

Frank snapped his fingers in front of Joel's face. "Earth to Joel. What happened to the drinks we wanted?"

"The bar was busy so I just ordered a couple of pitchers."

The other men grumbled.

"It's on me."

"Hey, all right." Frank slapped his palm on the table. "Drink up, men, Joel's buying."

Joel sat in his chair with his eyes glued to Colleen. After so many years of fantasizing about her, she sat within twenty feet of him. And she didn't say a damn word.

Betting Hearts

© *2006 Dee Tenorio*

Available now from Samhain Publishing.

He's never lost a bet in his life but she's playing for keeps!

Cassandra Bishop's boyfriend is back. Only problem is…she doesn't want anything to do with him. Or his new fiancée. What the confirmed tomboy would like is to wring his neck. She might have done it, too, if he hadn't filled her in on the embarrassing truth that he'd left her at the altar because she wasn't woman enough to satisfy him. Her pride nearly settled for punching him in the nose…until she thought of something better—proving him wrong.

High on Burke Hallifax's list of cataclysmic nightmares is having to look at his best friend as a real female. But when her ex-fiancé makes his wedding a personal vendetta against Cass, Burke has no choice but to bet everything on her ability to out hot-girl the competition. Unfortunately, the entire town is betting as well—on whether Burke and Cass can pull off the makeover of the century…without losing their hearts in the process.

"This isn't your night, Sel," Alice Panyon crowed to her husband a few hours later. She pulled in her third pot of the night with a smoky laugh.

"It's always my night, angel."

Cass smiled at the pair of them, the most improbable couple in all of Rancho Del Cielo. Where Selvyn Panyon was probably born in jeans and leather, Alice was the epitome of a debutante; cool, blonde and perfect. Ironically, Sel grew up to be a world-renowned artist while Alice was a retired firefighter. They were probably the happiest couple in town, too, with one little girl and another baby due to make an appearance sometime in the next few weeks. Not that a high, round belly kept Alice from stretching her arms around a pile of multicolored chips and chortling greedily.

Sel smoothed a wisp of Alice's white-blonde hair behind her ear, a gesture so intimate and familiar, Cass looked at the cards with a sense of guilt at having watched. Even jealousy. No one ever touched her like that.

But *someone* would.

Like a vow, the sentence ran through her mind as the cards ran through her fingers. When she did lift her eyes again, it wasn't to spy on Alice and Sel, or to see what May Belle and Jimmy were conspiring about this time, or even if Ben Friedly was trying to swipe another handful of popcorn from the bowl on the counter. It was to look at Burke as she shuttled cards around the table.

He hadn't made eye contact all evening but she concentrated on him until he couldn't avoid her any more. A deep blue, Burke's eyes were those of a man who thought, probably too much. He did everything deep in his head; math, bills, itinerary, designs for the cars he rebuilt from heaps. In the span of two minutes, the man could mentally take apart an entire engine and put it back together using all the pieces. Didn't take him much longer in real life either. His entire life was about plan of attack. If anyone should appreciate her setting a goal, it would be Burke. Normally.

Right now, she could tell he was thinking too much again. Chomping at the bit to get the evening's game over with so he could send her home with a pat on the head before having to discuss "the femininity plan". Well, she'd just have to get around that, now wouldn't she?

"Dealer's choice. Five-card stud, aces high, favor game. Showdown rules."

There were a few grumbles around the table, but no one complained about the game choice. Favor games were where you had to bet a favor instead of chips. Showdown rules meant in the case of only two players still holding, they could request a favor instead betting one. Burke eyed her suspiciously before reaching to the breakfast bar for the phone pad of paper and a pen. Cass gave him her best smile.

He almost knocked his chair over.

She stifled a laugh and set the leftover deck in front of herself. Carefully, she looked at her cards. Two queens, two aces and a deuce. She fought the urge to smile again as she lay down her deuce and slid it over to Jimmy. Burke was so going to lose.

They passed the pad around and by the time it made a full circle, the pot held a portrait sketch, a casserole, a lawn mowing, three free gallons of milk, a free dinner from Shaky Jakes and a Garth Brooks CD. Cass scowled. Damn, she better win this hand.

Right before she was about to call, Burke said he wanted to raise. He scribbled over the rights to his kitchen radio.

Fine, she could play dirty, too. She wrote her note and tossed it into the pot.

Jimmy leaned over and read her rotten handwriting by squinting one eye. "A date?"

"Gotta have one to take to Luke's wedding, don't I?"

She could have dropped a pin on the carpet and heard it snag.

Finally, Jimmy coughed. "Most of us here are married, CB. 'Cept Burke. You sure you wanna drag him to a wedding?" *In other words, are you sure you want to go to the wedding?*

"Pass me off to someone. You meet more people than I do, Jimmy. I'm sure Sel could find someone if it came down to it. Alice and May Belle keep trying to set me up with people, so there's no problem there."

Sel gave his wife a worried glance. Alice shrugged. What else was she supposed to do? It was true.

"What am I supposed to do with it?" Burke's baritone demanded.

Cass made herself shrug. "I don't know. Use it?"

His brows crashed together hard enough to clang.

"Give it to one of the guys at the shop. Pawn me off on a customer. Whatever you want."

"You're going to let us hand you off to some stranger?" Alice asked, each word enunciated with care, eyes darting from Cass to Burke and back. Cass nodded, waiting for the sign that Burke was paying attention.

There it was, the twitch of his eye when he thought she was doing something stupid. Reverse psychology was invented for Burke Halifax. No way would he let her go on a date with some stranger he didn't know. Even if he had to suffer himself.

Cass prepared herself for a hell of a game.

* * * * *

He should have throttled her while she was sleeping. Should have let her get pneumonia by sleeping on his front porch in the rain. He should have done anything but let her play poker tonight. The evil gleam in those green eyes warned she was about to be more trouble than she was worth but did he listen? No, of course not. That would have made sense. Now he was stuck watching the brat try to make him wriggle like a worm on a hook.

"Your bet, Jimmy." Cass blinked innocently at the older man on her left. *Ha! If she's innocent, I'm the mayor of Munchkinland.*

Jimmy slipped a glance over to Burke, who knew he didn't have to bother shaking his head. Jimmy ran the only grocery in town. He survived Korea, thirty-five years of marriage, two children, and most recently four years of marriage to May Belle. The man knew when to throw in the cards.

May watched her husband, shrugged and tossed down her five as well. "Sorry, CB, Burke looks about ready to bust a vein. If I set you up, we have to do it discreetly."

May Belle's main clientele were gamblers and gossips. If they did it, they'd be doing it over his dead body.

CB smiled, nodding her head like a queen. Of course. She was getting what she wanted.

Sel leaned forward to look around Alice's abundant stomach to check with Burke like Jimmy had before him. "I do know this one guy—"

"No, you don't, honey." Alice splayed her hand over Sel's cards and laid them on the table. Hers quickly followed suit. "And neither do I."

God, she better not be in on whatever CB was up to. Burke would hate to get angry with a pregnant woman.

He stared down at his own cards and wondered if he could beat her. They might only be fives, but it was hard to beat a three of a kind. He decided to risk it. All he had to do was take her bet and never call her on it. Easy as pie. "Call."

"You can't call."

"What? Why?"

"Showdown rules. It's just you and me now. I get to request a favor from you."

If she said even one damn word about finding her femininity, he was going to kill her and let the coroner look for it. Wrap both hands around that long neck of hers and squeeze till she popped. No one could convict him, either. Through gritting teeth he made himself ask, "Fine. What do you want?"

Cats with cream didn't look as pleased with themselves. She licked her lips, startling a rise out of him that had no business rising. You'd think his desire to do her in might have the smallest effect on him. At least his temper should have tamped the problem. It probably would have, but his worst nightmare began right before his eyes.

Cass leaned forward, wet lips pursed and pink, and said the words a man should never hear from his best friend. "It's simple, Burke. I want you to make me a woman."

Printed in the United States
58127LVS00003B/1-150

9 781599 982656